GUILTY BY CIRCUMSTANCE

Ron Fowler

TORNOW - COUNTRY MAP
(1) MCKENZIE, ELMER BODIES FOUND. (2) SIMPSON'S
OLD CAMP FIVE. (3) TORNOW HOMESTEAD, LOG CABIN.
(4)BAUER HOMESTEAD. (5) TORNOW LAKE. (6) SITE OF FORMER
PILLASHAK CABIN. (7) GROVE CEMETARY

(SCALE IS APPX.
ONE-INCH = THREE
MILES)

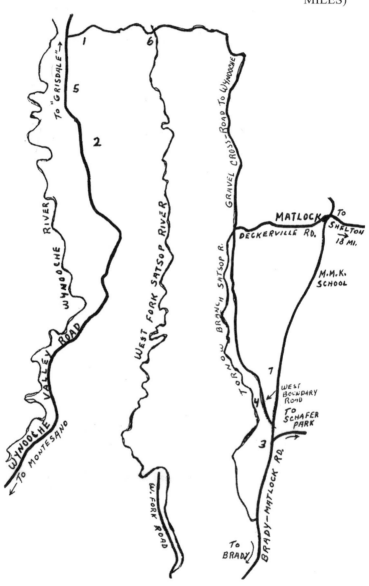

Guilty *by* Circumstance

The Troubled Life of Northwest Outlaw John Tornow

A Historical Novel By

RON FOWLER

Other Books by Ron Fowler:

Me N Pete

Self-Publishing the Write Way

The Valsetz Star

Seventh Printing

Library of Congress Catalog Card Number: 97-90804
ISBN: 0-9654479-1-X

Printed by Gorham Printing, Rochester, Washington

Copies of this book may be obtained by sending $14.95,
(WA residents only, add appropriate WA sales tax)
plus $1.00 shipping and handling to:
Fowler Freelance, 1371 Ranier Loop NW, Salem, OR, 97304.
Or contact the author at (503) 585-5479 or
FowlerRon@msn.com

FRONT COVER PICTURE: This contemporary monument was erected on John Tornow's grave at the Grove Cemetery near Matlock in June, 1987. It was designed, installed and contributed by Marty Schmid, owner of Harbor Monument in Aberdeen. Tom Roberson, composer of the "Ballad of John Tornow" assisted in the monument's development.

The beautiful slab of Ashland gray, Northwest granite was quarried in Oregon, weighing nearly one-half ton. The new monument replaced a small stone bearing simply the initials, "J.T." which had been the only marker on the forest fugitive's gravesite for many years.

Book design by Kathy Campbell

Dedication

Guilty by Circumstance is dedicated to the supportive board members of the Mary M. Knight Historical Program in Matlock whose input contributed immeasurably to the publication of this book. The diligent volunteer efforts of these local residents have produced an excellent museum collection of historical memorabilia of the area, including Tornow family records.

Foreword

Guilty By Circumstance is a fictionalized account of an actual historical event that occurred during the early 1900's in the Pacific Northwest wilderness.

*   *   *

Most primary incidents, characters and dates have been documented through fifty years of research. Some events, descriptions, and dialogue have been fabricated out of necessity. The fictitious timber baron, John Kennedy, has been created by the author to interject compassion and tenderness into an otherwise brutal and bloody chronicle of history.

*   *   *

Discretion has been exercised to assure that no person or character, dead or alive, has been unduly miscredited or maligned where historical validation does not exist. Decisions of guilt or innocence are left to the reader's judgment.

Prologue

The intriguing John Tornow story first attracted my attention when I was a fledgling reporter for the small town weekly newspaper in Montesano, Washington. It was the war years, mid–1940's, more than half-a-century ago. At various times during those intervening years, I have researched, interviewed and written about the forest loner who evaded capture around 1913 in the wilderness of Western Washington for over nineteen months. To the best of my knowledge, "Guilty By Circumstance" is the first full-length book on this saga.

John Tornow was one of five sons and one daughter, raised by Daniel Fritz Tornow and Louisa Tornow, who immigrated from Germany to Washington State (then Washington Territory) around 1870. The early settlers homesteaded a 160–acre section in the upper Satsop River valley near today's community of Matlock.

At the age of nine, John almost died from a serious bout with black measles. The attending country doctor cautioned the parents that the accompanying high fever could leave the youngster with an affliction of mind or body.

As a teenager, his only noticeable impairment was an aversion towards people. Young John became a true introvert, preferring a solitary existence in the wild, opposed to living in civilization.

John adored his sister Minnie, who married a neighboring countryman, Henry Bauer, in 1885. They raised four children, two girls and twin boys, John and William, born in 1892.

On September 3, 1911, the twin Bauer nephews of John Tornow were murdered by an unknown assailant while on a bear hunt near the family farm. In the vicinity, lawmen discovered a crude lean-to shack known to have been occupied by Tornow on occasion.

Disregarding John's known fondness for his nephews and their mother, his sister, the county posted a reward for his apprehension on grounds the sheriff wanted to question him regarding the murders.

The forest loner had earlier declared his abhorrence of civilization and humankind, vowing to forever live his preferred lifestyle alone in the wilderness. He became irritated with people, including relatives, who tried to force him back into society. He warned them to leave him alone.

From time to time, sheriff's posses were dispatched into the rugged mountains to bring Tornow in for questioning. He became a master of elusiveness until one day in March, 1912, when Deputy Colin McKenzie and Game Warden Al Elmer stumbled onto his crude hideout in the wilds of the Olympic Mountains. Pushed to his limit, the woods creature killed the two pursuers.

Most major incidents and characters in the book are factual, documented from reliable newspaper articles of the day plus library, museum and eye witness accounts.

Obviously, I have reconstructed conversation and minor events, as I believe would have occurred under the circumstances. In so doing I have given consideration to the known, and assumed predisposition and personality of each individual.

For inserting the fictional John Kennedy and several minor, unproven incidents, I apologize to the purist history buffs and disciples of bona fide Tornow memorabilia. I believe the introduction of this novelistic material will significantly enhance the reader's enjoyment.

Careful review of the reported friction that developed between

John Tornow and his brother, Edward, led me to believe the boys were involved in one-upmanship with each other. Edward, being the youngest son, was conditioned and expected to receive most favored treatment from the parents. Following John's near-death experience from the black measles, that attention was shifted away from Edward and heaped onto John as the "special child." Losing that warm and cozy parental favoritism undoubtedly had a negative impact on the youngest sibling's psyche. The jealousy resurfaced in later years culminating in the infamous killing of each other's pet hounds.

In 1963 I had the pleasure of meeting and spending considerable time with Upper Satsop pioneer, Albert Kuhnle. He related many alleged eye-witness accounts of the Tornow episode. On a bright and sunny spring afternoon, Kuhnle led me to Tornow Lake, even pointing out the preserved foot-log that led to the island and rustic lean-to where John and his father allegedly camped on occasion. During the ensuing interviews, Kuhnle showed me the .30–.30 Winchester rifle he said was carried by a deputy killed by John Tornow.

Several reports indicate there was a running feud between Henry Bauer, husband of the Tornow daughter, Minnie, and the other Tornow family members. At about the time the Bauer twin boys were murdered, or shortly after, Henry seemed to have mysteriously disappeared. None of the reports mentioned his presence later than 1911.

In my opinion, John Tornow was only *Guilty by Circumstance* in the murders of John and William Bauer. From the book, readers will individually arrive at their own conclusions.

I wish to express my appreciation to the many individuals who provided input necessary for publication of this book.

—Ron Fowler

The Fritz Tornow family posed for this picture taken against the still-standing log cabin wall. Probably taken around 1893. Standing, L to R: Albert, John, Minnie, Fred, William. Seated, L to R: Louisa, Edward, Fritz. (Photo courtesy of Ted Rakoski.)

Chapter One

"GRAB THREE RIFLES OFF THE GUN RACK," I YELLED AT CHARLEY. "No, no, not a scattergun. We ain't gonna get that close to John Tornow, leastways not if you wanta live to tell stories to your grandkids."

I ain't superstitious but I was hoping 1913 wasn't gonna be a bad year for me. I'm Deputy Sheriff Giles Quimby and my boss, Sheriff Schelle Mathews, told me to get a couple of deputies and hightail it into the thick timber country north of here to look for a killer who's been on the loose for nineteen months.

I knew in my bones this was gonna be a dangerous job. If I let myself think about it, I might fret and wonder if I had enough gumption to lead this posse. But what the hell! I'd chased outlaws before. If worse came to worst it ain't that big a deal. Got no family, nobody to stew about me if I don't make it back.

"We'd best take plenty of ammo," I barked at Deputies Charley Lathrop and Louie Blair as I grabbed handcuffs and my sheath knife and stuffed them into my beat-up old packsack.

"This Tornow's good. He's damned good. Already killed four, maybe more that ain't been found yet. Never knew what happened to them two prospectors that disappeared up in the Olympic Mountains last year."

My two deputy partners busied themselves at their desks in the sheriff's office in Montesano, Washington, Chehalis County seat, population 2,000, located about ninety miles southwest of Seattle.

As they laced up their scruffy, hightop leather logger's boots, I felt they were well chosen for this dangerous job. Both deputies were fur trappers, wilderness wise, crack shots and scared of nothin'. Charley had only one good eye, but he was a better shot than most with two good eyes. "T'was the other one I'd close for aimin' anyway," he once told me.

"Where we headin', Giles?" Louie asked as he leaned over and aimed a brown stream at the corner spittoon.

"Schelle says this guy he met on the train to Tacoma told him about a little lake east of the oxbow bend of the Wynooche River. Looked to him like somebody had been livin' there in a lean-to shack on a tiny island in the middle of the lake."

"Hell, that's miles from nowhere," Louie said as he shouldered one of the .30 calibre, lever-action rifles. "We're gonna have ourselves a hike."

Getting ready for this manhunt reminded me of my days in the army during the Spanish-American war of '98. I thought back about the dangerous times we had there with the enemy shootin' at us. At least Tornow was just one man. But he was one helluva man. Practically raised himself in the wild, like an animal. Tornow stood over six-feet tall and weighed two-hundred pounds. Me and the boys were all runts compared to him. None of us would go over a hundred-fifty, even after a big grange, potluck dinner. Short and tough, all three of us could handle ourselves in a fight. It wouldn't be our first and I hoped not our last.

Lookin' around the room, I checked one last time to make sure we weren't forgettin' nothin'. Our office in the new Chehalis County courthouse was kind of bare bones. No fancy stuff. Four wooden desks and chairs, one crank-handle telephone, a single, bare electric bulb hung from a brown cord in the middle of the room, faintly lighting up the dull-brown walls. Our scarred, wooden gunrack stood in the corner. It held the county's total arsenal of law and order weapons, now showing three empty places alongside the other Winchesters. As Charley closed and locked the cabinet, I got a strong whiff of heavy gun oil, an old familiar smell that often reminded me of the perils I had faced before.

I pulled the chain that turned out the light and back-heeled the door shut behind me. Walking down the dark hallway to the jail exit, Charley piped up, "We'd best stop at Veysey's General Store and get some grub to take along."

"Glad you mentioned it," I said, "been hurryin' so fast I would have plumb forgotten about eats."

"We takin' extra clothes?" Louie asked, buttoning up his heavy mackinaw jacket and pulling down his stained, slouch hat.

"Naw, I don't think we'll be gone that long, maybe a week, shouldn't need more'n an extra pair of socks."

"Well, I won't wear my new overalls," Louie joked, a bravado grin spreading across his weather-worn face. "Wouldn't want Tornow to get 'em. I heard he stripped the bodies of Deputies Elmer and McKenzie after he killed 'em."

"Hell, Louie, you needn't worry. He ain't gonna come after you. You're too damned ugly." Charley laughed as he ducked a playful jab from his fellow deputy.

We stepped outside to a dull-gray, spring morning. Heavy black clouds scudded across the depressing sky, a sure sign of rain. The dirt parking lot behind the courthouse was shiny slick from the last shower that had passed through. But the air smelled fresh and clean, scrubbed good by Mother Nature.

"Let's take the Ford," I proposed as I carried my packsack and rifle towards the parked police car. "We'll drive that miserable damned road up the Satsop River to Matlock. Then we can get a ride into old camp five on the logging railroad. Ain't no roads beyond

Matlock. From the camp we'll be on shank's mare."

"I gotta stop at the house for a second," Charley said, throwing his duffle in the backseat of the black Model-T. Need to pickup a couple 'a things, maybe grab a few spuds, and I'll take my Airedale if it's o.k."

"Sure, bring him along," I replied, buttoning down the isinglass side curtains on the driver's door. "Chief is a good tracker and we might need him before we're through."

We piled into the Ford patrol car that was parked on the rain-slickened lot. "Get out and crank for me, Louie," I said, sliding behind the monstrous, wooden steering wheel. I could feel the cold dampness of the stiff, leather seats through my wool cruiser trousers. Just two spins of the crank handle and the four-cylinder engine sprang to life with a rattling wheeze. I adjusted the spark and gas levers and let the engine warm up. The choking exhaust smell came up through the wooden floorboard cracks.

As we waited, a blustery wind pushed the dark clouds overhead. Each of us was lost in our own thoughts about this assignment. I wanted to make sure I hadn't forgotten any details. One small blunder could mean the difference between life and death for all of us. I knew the sheriff was thinking about appointing a chief deputy and I sure wanted that job. I wanted it bad. If I didn't screw up on this manhunt, I would be in line for the promotion.

I was jarred from my thoughts by a couple of loud bangs as the Ford backfired. I readjusted the spark lever. "Well, boys, are you ready?"

Hearing no reply I eased the car onto the narrow, gravelled street leading downtown from the courthouse. Turning sharply I heard the rifles in the backseat slide onto the floor with a helluva clatter.

"Not loaded are they?" I checked with Charley who was sitting in back.

"No, everything's Jake."

We were headed south towards town when a bright flash of dancing, spring lightning silhouetted the early-budding branches of maples lining the vacant street. A sharp wind gust flurried the leafless, red twigs and branchlets of the young red maple trees that stood a solitary vigilance alongside the gravel road.

Soon I could smell the warm scent of ozone that floated in the air after the lightning discharge. Out to the west an even darker pall loomed across the horizon, a sure bet we were in for heavy weather. The dismal day dampened my spirits. Was it an omen, I wondered, or perhaps a deadly prophecy?

Down at the next corner, an empty farm wagon moved slowly across the rutted intersection, reins in the hands of a hunched driver, who was coaxing a bedraggled-looking brown mare.

I turned onto Pioneer Street and brought the Ford to a shuddering halt in Charley's front yard. He hopped out and disappeared inside the two-story wooden house that seemed to cry out for lack of a paint job, but then most houses in town looked that way. Paint jobs were expensive. I waved to Joe Deane, the town druggist, who rode his bicycle by on his way to work.

The erratically vibrating engine shook me from side to side as we waited for Charley. "Guess we got enough gas to get to Matlock," I absentmindedly mumbled to nobody in particular.

"I filled the tank last night," Louie commented, "but it won't be enough to get back."

"We'll worry about that later."

As I again thought about going in after John Tornow, the muscles in my neck began to tighten, and I felt a cold hand grip my heart. Maybe it would help to talk about it. "Schelle told me that we should hike into the old Pillashak homestead, use it as a base camp," I told Louie. "The lake's supposed to be a few miles northwest of there in heavy timber."

"This weather don't look none too good," Louie commented as he wiped steam from the inside of the thin, isinglass windows.

"We'll need our rain slickers in that Oxbow country. Rains cats and dogs up there. Surely does. I read where they had more than 120 inches last year. Some homesteader measured it. Hell's bells, that's over ten feet of rain. A fella could drink standin' up."

The door soon opened and Charley's lively Airedale leaped into the backseat, his pink, wet tongue dangled loosely from his mouth which seemed to form a friendly smile. Charley threw in a small tote bag and climbed up beside Chief. "Sorry to keep you guys waitin'. I met a friend of mine and had to kiss her goodbye."

"You had time enough to do more than kiss her," Louie said with a grin. I struggled the Model-T's stiff steering wheel around the corner to Main street and pulled up in front of Veysey's store.

It began to rain a gully washer; cloud burst; downpour; a real rain. The monsoon kind we often get in Western Washington State in April.

I turned off the ignition and the clankety engine groaned to a halt. As I stepped onto the Ford's running board, I tried to avoid a sloppy mud puddle in the crude street. Charley and Louie also hopped out. Chief was left alone sitting up like a sentinel in the backseat, enjoying his new guard dog responsibilities.

"Let's get a few provisions, enough to last a week or so," I said as we hurried through the downpour and stepped over the fast-filling mudholes.

"Yeah, and I need a couple of plugs of Star-chew," Louie added.

The portly storekeeper, his white apron clean for a change, greeted us at the door. Must 'a been a slow day.

"Hi fellas, you headin' out?"

"Yeah, we got some huntin' to do," I told him without telling him much. We bought bacon, coffee, flour and hardtack.

"Put this stuff on the sheriff's account," I told the storekeeper as I loaded the food into a gunnysack.

"Not the tobacco," Louie interrupted. "That's for my tab." I'll be in to square up with you when I get paid next month."

As we left the store I waved at Bob Crinklaw who was driving his horse and buggy towards the livery stable. There were a few cars in town but most folks still used horses to get around. Like an endless chain of tiny lakes, small puddles of muddy rainwater had begun to dot the hard-packed Main Street. Few people stirred. The rainstorm had chased most everyone indoors.

The Model-T's warm engine came to life with Louie's single turn of the crank handle. Bouncing the Ford between chuckholes, I turned east out of town to what would become our date with destiny.

Within just a couple of blocks, the gravel road became narrow, just wide enough for one car or wagon. There were turnouts every so often. If we met someone, one of us would have to pull off the road and let the other rig go past. This was the main highway between Olympia and Washington's western coast but on this drizzly April morning there was almost no traffic. "They're runnin' cars on these roads built for horses," I grumbled.

The road followed the river-bottom where a few stump ranchers tried to scratch out a living in the tangled mass of timber and thick brush. They'd cleared small patches of land where they tried to grow meager crops, raise some livestock and a few kids. They grew, shot, or caught what food they needed. It was a hard life, too hard for most.

The Ford's rackety engine became even louder as I gunned her up to nearly thirty miles an hour. At this speed I had to fight the steering wheel to stay out of the gravel ruts. Gripping the wheel, I glanced over at Louie in the front seat beside me. His wide-brimmed, stained Stetson was pulled down over his eyes as he tried to catch forty winks despite the rattling, bouncy ride. I felt comfortable with him along on this manhunt. He was dependable, an excellent woodsman. In his spare time he trapped for furs in the mountains north of town. If we got into deep trouble I knew he would stand and fight.

Suddenly I heard a strange noise. It was almost louder than the Ford's engine. I looked around. Then I saw it. Charley was sprawled in the backseat, head back, mouth wide open, snoring up a storm. Curled beside him, Chief was also asleep, his nose tucked warmly under his tummy. I shook my head in disbelief. How could these two guys sleep with all the noise and cold air whistling in around the flimsy side curtains?

Charley was another part-time trapper who had lived mostly around the lumber town of Shelton. Although he was blind in one eye, it hadn't hurt his marksmanship and he was completely at home in the deep timber. I told myself we'd need every ounce of his know-how if we met up with John Tornow.

We soon arrived at the turnoff road up the Satsop valley. The new roadway was even rougher than the one we had left. Louie sat up from his slouched nap position. "How much farther?" he asked, belching and yawning at the same time.

"We've just started up the valley," I replied, "sure hope this damned road is open all the way to Matlock. We got almost twenty miles to go."

"Did you know that old Sol Simpson got his start in loggin' around Matlock in '95?" Louie inquired.

"Yeah, that was eighteen years ago and Simpson's still goin' strong," I replied.

It seemed the road got worse and worse. Some places were only gravelled through the swamps. No turnouts—we'd just have to take our chances if we met somebody. Louie went back to sleep. Amazing.

Alone with my thoughts, the steering wheel, and the treacherous road, I couldn't help but feel jittery about going into the uncharted wilderness against this outlaw fugitive. The woods were his bailiwick, his home. He knew the country from having lived in it for many years, and he claimed it as his own. For nineteen months out there he'd played cat and mouse with the men sent to capture him. And when they got too close, when they threatened his backwoods way of living, he killed with precision, quickly and deadly. Not a very pleasant thought just before going in after him.

Damn you, Tornow. Why'd you have to go and kill them fellows? You ain't no killer. Why couldn't you just leave 'em be? Now, he had me talking to myself.

We crossed over the Satsop river on a rickety wooden bridge as the rain continued to dimple the windshield. Even the loud clatter of the span's loose planks didn't waken my two deputies, nor the dog. Beneath us roiled the coffee-colored water from the storm-drenched Olympic Mountains whose snow-capped peaks and lower foothills run-off had raised the normally peaceful little river to near flood stage.

We chugged past haunted Henry's homestead and onto Schafer's plateau where the muddy road wound through a stand of virgin Douglas firs. Once again my thoughts drifted back to our manhunt. I was angry that I couldn't block it out of my mind, that I couldn't think of more pleasant things, but the sheriff's words on the telephone the previous evening kept coming back to haunt me like a bad dream.

"Giles, I want you to go up to that lake and look around. Try to determine if Tornow is there. Under no circumstances should you fellas go in after him. He's too dangerous. If it appears that he's there, we'll send in a bigger posse to get him. Please be very, very careful. Don't spook him. You're not only my best deputy, you're also my favorite brother-in-law."

Original Tornow homestead now owned by Mr. and Mrs. Bud Larson who purchased it in 1966. Tornow's first log cabin is at left. Around the turn of the century, Tornow built the larger house in the foreground, later relocated and reshaped.

Sure, I thought, easy for Schelle to say that. He was safe in the city. But, if we go into the lake just to have a look, it's likely Tornow will know we're there. Then what? Be careful, Schelle said. But how exactly do you do that around a half-crazed man on the run?

I slowed for the steep downhill on Fryin' Pan mountain and we soon came to the Tornow home-place beside the road. Charley and Louie roused from their naps. Yawning, Chief sat up beside his master. "That's where it all began," I said, pointing to the small log cabin behind the newer looking house.

"Yep, that's where old Fritz and Louise Tornow homesteaded in 1879 and first lived in that little shack. Did it on a shoestring," Charley added. "Hardy stock them rugged Germans." The homestead was in a large clearing, surrounded by towering fir trees that seemed hell-bent to reach to the clouds. A few stumps remained, dead reminders of trees felled to form the cabin, and several farm buildings. Fences were neatly built of small poles, the cheapest and most readily available material. Dried, upright stalks of dormant fireweed grew among the stumps.

"Didn't I hear tell that John nearly died with the black measles when he was just a young 'un?" Louie asked.

"That's the low-down," I replied. "They say the sickness is what caused him to be just a trifle bit off plumb."

"Yeah, but then I heard wasn't nothin' wrong with his head," Louie said. "Most of the trouble was between him and one of his brothers, they say."

"Well, the sickness sure didn't hurt his shootin' eye none," I added as we passed the Tornow barn and small pasture where a couple of Holsteins grazed on the stubby grass. "I've heard tell he can light match heads at a hunnert feet with that old U.S. .30 rifle of his."

"If we run across him, we'd best try to outsmart him, 'stead of tryin' to outshoot him," Charley said wisely.

Within a mile, we came to a dirt side road that turned off west towards the middle fork of the Satsop River.

"The Bauer place is just a short piece down that road," I told the boys. "Minnie, the oldest Tornow child, married old Henry Bauer. They was the parents of the twin boys John was supposed to have killed about two years ago. I still have my doubts he done it though."

Louie opened the side curtain a crack and spat a tobacco stream outside, wiping his mouth on the sleeve of his wool jacket. "Yeah, I went up with the posse when we was huntin' for the Bauer boys after they didn't come home that day. Finally found their bodies in a shallow grave 'bout a mile from the house. Mighty peculiar circumstances if you'd ask me," Louie said. "Couple of other fellas looked more suspicious to me than John Tornow. Take that other brother for instance. The twins' pa, old man Bauer, could 'a done it too."

"How about that four-flusher timber baron who has been hangin' around the Bauer place? What's his name, Giles?"

"You mean John Kennedy? Yeah. Some will tell you he had plenty reason for shootin' the twins, bad blood between him and old Henry. I met him once. He's a high-falutin' son of a buck, too fancy for my likes. But they say Minnie's kinda sweet on him since her old man disappeared."

As the road narrowed, becoming even rougher than before, I could tell we were getting close to Matlock. We'd park there and try to catch the logging train into the timber camp between the Satsop and Wynooche Rivers.

I could feel a knot clenching tightly in the pit of my stomach. We'd soon be out there, I thought to myself. We'd be just the three of us against this outlaw who they say could sneak up on you in the forest, quiet as a ghost. Then I began to think back about my time in the war. I'd never told anyone about how those Spanish soldiers came rushing up to our post. Too many of 'em, there was. Me and the boys got scared tryin' to think what to do, so we just had to hightail it. Saved our skins but felt bad afterwards. Later on we got even with them Spaniards. Surely we did.

Soon I saw a long white building down the middle of the road. That would be the Matlock General Store right alongside the railroad tracks. That's where the road ended.

"This little burg sure ain't grown none in the past few years," Louie said as we slowed to park in front of the store.

"Look at them ramshackle cabins, hardly fit to live in."

"Ain't nothin' much here 'cept stumps after the loggers cut out most of the timber and moved on," Charley added.

It was a quiet little community. A few shacks, no trees, just an endless cemetery of bleached, dead stumps as far as the eye could see. The stumps were six, maybe eight feet across, grim reminders of a once tall forest that had been reaped by the faller's "misery whip" steel hand saws.

"I'll go into the store and find out when the next train is due," I said, turning off the ignition and stepping onto the Model-T's running board. I glanced quickly at the gray sky and noted the rain had stopped. The mountain air smelled fresh and pure like it had been washed clean by the spray from a misty waterfall.

My deputies got out of the car, stretching and yawning from the long drive. Charley's tawny, brown dog hopped out and began looking for a tree. Then he decided one of the Model T's tires would be just as good.

There wasn't much business for the store. It had been left behind by the advancing timber companies. A covered porch ran the length of the front, its floor planks chewed, as if by termites, from decades of logger's spiked boots. A sleek chestnut bay, head drooped, stood patiently at the hitchin' rail near the porch.

The store manager, dressed in white apron, shirt sleeves held in place with bright blue garters, sporting a classy handlebar mustache, greeted us at the door. I noticed he was eyeballing the silver stars pinned to our jackets. "Good afternoon, Sheriff. What can I do for you boys?"

Matlock was on the edge of my jurisdiction so I didn't get up here very often. "I'm Giles Quimby, Chehalis county deputy sheriff. These are my deputies, Charley and Louie. We need a lift to camp five. When will the next train be comin' through?"

"Sounds like you're chasin' after John Tornow, huh? I sure wouldn't want to be in your shoes. The train? Should be along in about an hour."

"We're headin' for the old Pillashak homestead. Do you suppose the train will take us into camp?"

Wiping off the lid of a huge, wooden pickle barrel, the manager said, "Seein' that you're lawmen, I reckon they'll accommodate you. Kind of a coincidence you're headin' for the Pillashak. Old One-arm Olson, the Swedish prospector, came through a few days ago, said he seen John Tornow near that homestead.

Yessir, even said he talked with John. Course, that old galoot ain't too reliable, drunk most of the time. He had a jug of moonshine tucked under his arm last I seen him."

It ain't often I can read a man's mind but glancing at my two deputies, I could tell what they were thinkin' after the storekeeper said John had been seen around the Pillashak. He could be out there anyplace. We could run into him along the trail; he might even be waiting in ambush.

Charley pursed his thin, weathered lips to speak but said nothing. Thinking to himself instead. The manager smiled at us, perhaps sensing our worries. Probably thankin' his lucky stars the worst he had to worry about was keepin' the kids out of the cracker bin.

"Hey, I got a pot of coffee on the stove, why don't you fellas sit a spell? You got a wait 'til the train shows up."

He walked us over to the middle of the building where a big cast iron, pot-bellied stove was throwing vapors of welcome heat into the musky-smelling room. A blue enameled coffee pot, big enough for a logging crew, sat on the stove-top perking out thin wisps of steam. It smelled good in the store, kind of a mixture of oakum, sorghum, moldy cheese and pickle juice.

These logs forming cabin walls are nearly in the same condition as when hand-hewn by Fritz Tornow in the 1870's.

24

The store-keep grabbed three tin cups off a tall wooden shelf and wiped them with his apron. He handed us a cup and poured steaming shots of a thick, black brew, not unlike used motor oil, and strong enough to melt spruce pitch. I'd bet it had been perkin' several days. We leaned back on a long, splintered wooden bench and enjoyed a few swigs of the manager's thick coffee. As I looked around the store, I noticed the tall shelves going all the way up to the ceiling. A sign hung in the middle of the room, "Everything from a needle to a locomotive." I could believe it. The shelves were stacked with a colorful collection of everything: bolts of gaudy cloth, cans and bottles of foodstuffs, lanterns, washboards, pots and pans, stove pipe. There was even a display of ladies girdles.

The storekeeper waited on a customer who bought a box of rifle cartridges. The fellow then mounted his saddle horse and rode down the middle of the muddy street. Shuffling over to where we sat, the clerk said, "You fellas can pile your totes on the front porch and wait for the train. It should be along any minute now."

We thanked him for the coffee and hurried out to the Ford. Chief was standing guard at the passenger's door, and he wagged his stubby tail as he saw us coming.

"Unload our stuff and I'll pull behind the store where the car'll be out of the way," I told the boys.

Our packsacks and rifles on the porch caught the attention of several curious townsfolk as they walked by. With our guns and badges, guess we did stick out like sore thumbs. Sort of like being on display in one of them wild west museums.

In just a few minutes, we heard the mournful train whistle shattering the silence of the peaceful little community. Like a steam-belching, black dragon, the Shay lokey soon came chugging around the bend and stopped in front of the store. It was pulling a long string of empty log flatcars coming from the mill in Shelton, heading back out to the woods for another load.

The train engineer stepped nimbly down the engine's worn, iron stairs and walked towards us. He was dressed in greasy, striped overalls and a worn, dark-blue engineer's cap. As he came up the porch steps, I introduced myself. "Could we hitch a ride to camp five? We need to hike into the old Pillashak homestead, lookin' for John Tornow."

Chief cautiously sniffed the engineer's trouser leg then turned away like he'd smelled something whiffey. Wiping his nose on the back of his soiled jacket, the engineer replied, "Sure, I'll go real slow when I pull out so you can hop aboard the caboose when it comes past. Just go in and tell the brakeman who you are. Goin' after John, huh? Funny thing, I saw him last summer. As we came around a bend in the deep timber, there he stood all alone beside the track. Seemed harmless. He even waved at me."

"You can't tell about him," I answered. "Mark my word, several people have found out maybe he ain't so harmless."

The trainman went into the store and came out with a plug of dark brown chewing tobacco. Walking back to the engine, he bit off a corner of the hard, strong-smelling plug, chomped it soft 'til the juice ran between his teeth, and looked at us with a satisfied grin.

We'd piled all our stuff beside the track. "You guys will have to throw my packsack on board. It'll be all I can do to handle this mutt and get him on," Charley said.

I jumped at least a foot when the engineer gave two mighty blasts on the steam whistle. With a rattling lurch, the empty flatcars, cluttered with bits of tree bark, began to roll past. I found the combined smells of railroad axle grease, creosote, coal smoke and hemlock pitch to be surprisingly pleasant. The massive iron train wheels echoed click-clack as they rolled over a slit in a rail splice.

"Get ready," I said, "here comes the caboose."

We shouldered our rifles. Charley got hold of Chief in a bear hug. The dog's legs stiffened and stuck out like four wooden stilts. I grabbed up his packsack with my own and we jumped onto the iron steps of the rust-colored caboose as it slowly rolled by. Luckily, we all made it. Chief seemed to take it in his stride, like he hopped trains everyday.

The brakeman was dozing in his worn seat and sleepily waved us towards a bench across the aisle. The track twisted and turned, mostly through already logged, open country. A few stands of virgin timber had been by-passed by the persistent loggers. On only a few straight stretches did we see the locomotive that snaked fifty or sixty flatcars ahead of us. Soon we arrived at the logging camp and the end of the mainline.

Charley and Louie had joined the brakeman taking a brief nap. "O.K., boys," I said, picking up my pack and rifle, "time to go to work."

From here, several sets of temporary track twisted across hillsides into stands of 200-foot tall Douglas fir, Western red cedar and mountain hemlock. The logs were brought into camp and loaded onto flatcars for the mill. Bunkhouses, shop and storage buildings were located throughout the camp area. The railroad was the only way in, unless you wanted to walk.

A mustached, snoose chewing logger pointed out the trail that would take us out of camp to the abandoned homestead. It was midafternoon and it had quit raining but we could see that the brush and tree limbs were studded with sparkling droplets of water.

We put on our raincoats. Leaving camp, I led the way with Chief bounding ahead, then dropping back with his master. The trail passed through cut-over sections of open stump-land near camp. Shortly we entered the virgin forest that had not yet felt the bite of the logger's axe or saw. We were now in the foothills of the Olympic Mountains and the country became more rugged as we went further north. Steep hillsides dropped into deep ravines and dense underbrush where tinkly little creeks splashed merrily towards the rivers. Low-growing salal and red huckleberry bushes grew in a jungled thicket understory wherever narrow shafts of sunlight penetrated the forest canopy.

"Let's stay on our toes in this overgrown country, Tornow could be anywhere," Louie said, bringing up the rear on the trail. "Like lookin' for a needle in a haystack," he said, often casting a nervous glance behind him.

I knew Louie was right. With each step I felt we were moving closer to Tornow's bailiwick and farther away from ours. Civilization was behind us. There was nothing up ahead except wilderness and John Tornow. I worried. I worried a lot.

Later, as we hiked along the trail, Charley asked, "Anybody got the time?"

I pulled out my pocket watch tied to my trousers with a stout string. "Five o' clock."

"How much farther we got to go? It'll be dark soon."

"Schelle said he thought the homestead was about five miles from camp."

Dark clouds hid the sun but I noticed the light was growing dim under the deep forest cover. We walked a little faster.

Suddenly, Chief broke out ahead of me on the trail. He stopped, stiff-legged, his nose arrowed straight ahead like a pointer. I stopped short behind him.

"What's the matter?" Louie asked.

"Dog has picked up on somethin'." I heard the metallic click of rifle actions jacking live cartridges into the firing chambers. The boys weren't taking any chances.

Chief stood perfectly still like he was frozen to the trail. As my

Only a new roof has been added to the original Tornow log cabin.

heartbeat moved into high gear, I strained to pick up any sound from the thick jungle ahead. It was quiet behind me. I knew my partners were also listening. Very faintly I heard movement off to my right. Chief heard it too. He turned his head in that direction, ears at attention.

I stepped back and whispered to Charley, "Send him into the brush over there. I heard something."

Charley silently slipped past me and stooped beside the Airedale. "Get 'em," he commanded, pointing to the thicket. That was all the encouragement the dog needed. With a low growl he sprang off the trail like one of them gazelles and disappeared into the heavy timber. I lost sight of him but could hear him running through the underbrush.

Suddenly, looking down the trail into the deep shadows, I saw a figure leap out of the tangled thicket and take off out the path, running away from us. I smiled. It was a smile of relief. Chief had flushed a small, brown deer from the timber.

As I looked back at the boys, I saw they were smiling too. "Had us goin' there for a minute," Louie stammered. "But it was just a little black-tail."

Out ahead, Chief stood on the trail looking back at us. I could swear he had a look on his face that seemed to say, Didn't I do good? We continued towards the Pillashak as the shadows lengthened and darkness began to shroud the deep timber.

"How do we find it in the dark," Charley asked, climbing over a blow-down spruce sapling that had fallen across the path.

"They say the trail ends right at the abandoned cabin," I replied.

The blackness of nightfall came on us like someone had blown out a lantern. I became concerned. Could we find the shack in the dark? There was no moon. Chilling thoughts raced through my mind as we stumbled over boulders and limbs that we couldn't see in the inky darkness. It was my responsibility to lead the deputies to the cabin. What would Schelle say if I got us lost in this wilderness? Think, Giles, think, I kept repeating to myself.

Chief was now leading the way, smelling out the trail ahead of us. It was comforting to have him in front even though I couldn't see him most of the time. "It can't be much farther now," I said, trying to raise the deputies' morale as well as my own. Looking ahead, I could see a patch of sky that was a bit less than pitch black. It looked like a clearing. My spirits soared, the Pillashak would have to be in a clearing the homesteaders had cut. Maybe this was it.

In a few minutes, a faint black blob loomed up against the night sky. Soon we could see it had the outline of a building. "Guess we've found it," Charley said. "I knew we would." I tried to sound confident.

Feeling our way around the building we finally came to the door which was about three feet off the ground with no steps leading to it.

Chief furiously sniffed the low grass like he was on the hot trail of a scared rabbit. He'd found something. I reached up and pulled the latch-string to open the door. It wouldn't budge. I pushed against it and got it open enough to stick my head inside. As the door opened, the Airedale immediately went into his "pointer" position again. A low growl formed in his throat as he stared at the open door. Thinking what danger might be waiting for us inside, my mouth went dry as flour. Chief was upset. He knew what was in there.

"What is it, boy?" Charley asked, putting his hand on the dog's tawny muscular neck.

"Must be someone in there," Louie offered.

"Maybe just a skunk, or somethin'" I said.

I climbed up and peered through the half-open door, keeping low to the log floor. "Darker than blazes in here, can't see nothin'."

Charley dug around in his packsack feeling for a candle stub he'd thought to bring along. He struck a match and lit the wick, then gave me the candle. "Hand my rifle up, will you, Louie?"

I felt the cold steel of my Winchester, slipped a cartridge into the chamber and carefully slid the weapon onto the floor in front of me. I held my finger on the trigger as I slowly pushed the candle into the room.

"Whatcha see?" Louie impatiently asked.

I could hear Chief continuing to growl. It took a few seconds for my eyes to adjust to the dark room and the flickering light. Then the candle was too close and it blinded me so I shoved it off to one side. The tiny flame sent dim shafts of light dancing across the cabin walls and ceiling. I strained to make out any objects inside.

"It's still too damned dark," I told the boys. "Hell, this ain't workin', I'm gonna go in. Back me up Louie."

I leaned heavily against the door and forced it open enough to crawl through. On hands and knees, candle and rifle held apprehensively in front of me, I moved into the middle of the dirty cabin. It smelled dank and dusty with a faint trace of something sweet. I couldn't identify the unusual odor. As I got closer to the far wall I suddenly thought I saw a body lying on the floor. Were my eyes playing tricks on me? No, it was a body. The body of a man dressed in tattered, dirty clothes. He wasn't moving, must be either dead or sleeping.

"Come on in, boys, bring Chief." I heard my deputies climb up onto the floor and move forward on their hands and knees.

"The dog don't want no part of this," Charley said, handing me another candle. "What did you find?"

"There's the body of a man over near the far wall," I told him. "Take your candle and ease up on him. I'll crawl up from this other side. Louie can cover both of us from here." I got close enough to the lifeless form to poke him with my rifle barrel. Nothing. I shoved it hard into his gut. Then I heard a groan. Now with both candles we stood over the man as I tried to shake him awake. He finally came around, blinking his eyes, trying to figure out what was going on.

"Looks drunk to me," Charley said.

"Who are you?" I asked. "Name's Olson, who are you?"

Then we remembered the story about the prospector who had seen John Tornow in these parts. This was him alright.

"We're sheriff's deputies and we're gonna stay here tonight," I told him.

"That's o.k. by me, I'll go sleep in the back room. Do you boys have any booze with you?" he asked with a drunken slur.

"We don't carry that stuff when we're workin'."

Changing the subject, I asked, "Has John Tornow been around these parts lately?"

"John Tornow?" he replied. "Hee, hee, John Tornow's here. He's everywhere. Why he gave me a venison roast just last week. Or was it last month?" he asked, putting his hands to his head as if to stroke his brain into remembering.

"When was the last time you seen him?" I demanded, moving

closer to the old codger in my impatience.

"Seen him? I seen him maybe yesterday. He's my friend. You fellers ain't fixin' to hurt him, are you?" he cackled, his high-pitched voice scrapin' off the rough, log-hewn, cabin walls.

"No, of course not. We just want to talk with him." I gave up tryin' to get Olson to talk sense. The old codger crawled away into the darkness. I'm glad he knew where he was going. I couldn't see a thing over there.

"Let's scrounge up enough wood to get a fire goin' in that empty barrel," I said. Within a few minutes I coaxed a puny flame to life under a few chunks of dry wood that someone had left in the cabin. As the fire grew, the flames threw fingers of faint light on the unfinished log walls of the shanty.

"Look what I found," Charley said, picking up an empty gallon jug and smelling it. "Phew, that was rot-gut moonshine, but it's gone now."

"I could smell it when I first came into the room," I said.

We soon had bacon frying in an old pan and made coffee with water from a rain barrel out in the yard. Smelling the food, Chief finally wandered cautiously into the shack.

After our scrimpy supper, we sat on the floor with our backs against the wall and soaked up the little heat that came from the coals in the barrel. Me and Charley dug pipes out of our packsacks and lit up a bowl for an after-dinner smoke. Puffing a blue cloud, Charley said, "I been meanin' to ask you, Giles, what about that reward that's on Tornow's head? You know it's up to five thousand now, don't you?"

"Yeah, I know, but it don't concern me none. Schelle don't want us to chase Tornow down, just try to find out if he's at the lake."

"We go up and find out he's there, it's gonna be mighty temptin' not to go in after him," Louie said, biting off a chew of his tobacco plug. "A fella could retire on that kind of money. It's more mink skins than I could catch in a lifetime."

"Might be temptin' if you don't mind gettin' your head blowed off," I cautioned the boys. "The sheriff is sendin' Deputies Stormes and Elliott to rendezvous with us. If Tornow's at the lake we're gonna wait before we go in and get him. Safer that way. Sheriff's orders."

"I hunted a time or two with John, I think I could talk him into comin' out peacefully," Charley said, "I don't think he'd shoot me."

"Only one way to find out about that, and if you're wrong, you're gonna be dead-wrong," I told him. From out of the darkness we heard the loud snoring of the drunken prospector.

"Guess we'd better turn in too," I said. We spread our bedrolls on the dusty log floor. Chief stretched out his long, curly brown body between me and Charley and rested his head on his wet front paws. Best I could do for a pillow was the small sack of flour we'd bought.

"G'night fellas." I heard a mumble. Louie was already snoring.

Sleep didn't come quick enough for me, though. I laid there thinking about what we had ahead of us. Couldn't get it out of my

Bits of English-language newspaper used for insulation can still be found on interior walls of Tornow log cabin. Earliest date on papers was 1896.

mind. It now seemed like I'd have a tough time talkin' the boys out of goin' in after Tornow. Just the temptation of the damned money was enough. Don't they worry none about their lives? My thoughts drifted back to that day during the war when bullets were flying, and it had been so scary. What would happen tomorrow if we ran into Tornow? Could I face up to him? I wanted to demonstrate my courage in front of the deputies. And I kept thinkin' about that chief deputy job.

Morning came. We doused our fire after breakfast and hiked to the lake, finding it easy enough, just like Schelle had said. There was a lean-to shack on an island in the middle of the lake.

Louie smiled, "He's there, let's go." "No, no," I pleaded, "it's too dangerous. Besides, we got our orders. The sheriff says to wait for more men."

"I don't know about you, Giles," Charley said, "but me and Louie, we're goin' in after that reward money. You can wait here if you want."

I turned tail and ran down the trail. Headed straight back for the Pillashak, had to get away from there.

Suddenly I sat bolt upright, wide awake. Chief stared at me in the pre-dawn darkness with a wondering look. It had been a bad dream, a real nightmare. I felt damp, I'd been sweating, but thank God it had only been a dream, not for real. Laying back down on my flour pillow I was almost afraid to go back to sleep. Afraid of another nightmare. I laid awake the rest of the night, maybe dozed off for short catnaps a couple of times.

There was one small window in the shack, four panes, two of 'em had been busted out. I wondered how I could see this in the dark. Then I realized that the soft half-light of early morn was lighting up the room.

Pulling on my boots, I stood up and clearly saw the inside of the cabin for the first time. It wasn't much. A few scattered pieces of broken furniture, rusty cans and busted bottles, the old codger's empty jug, and lots of cobwebs.

"Come on boys, it's daylight in the swamp," I yelled.

Charley and Louie began to stir but Chief decided it was too early for him.

The sizzling bacon, campfire biscuits and burbling can of dark-brown coffee spun tasty odors throughout the room as we cooked our breakfast over the fire barrel.

I tried to convince the boys we needed to scout the lake and not carelessly go helter-skelter after Tornow. "The sheriff told me he was sendin' Stormes and Elliott to meet us here at the Pillashak today. We'd best not jump the gun. Let's wait for them."

"It'll take 'em two-three days to get here. Ain't no reason we should wait that long," Charley said. "Come on Giles, let's go, we'll be careful."

We packed up our stuff, leaving a few scraps of breakfast for One-arm Olson who staggered groggily into the barren room. Outside, the weather was getting better as patches of blue sky greeted us in the clearing that had been carved out of a stand of thick timber.

I tried to think of some way to keep the deputies from leaving but I couldn't. I didn't want to go, but I didn't want them to go alone. I knew we should wait. Charley and Louie just seemed to put the reward money ahead of risking their lives.

"Let's just follow the trail to the lake, take a quick look around, then come back and wait for Stormes and Elliott," I suggested.

"We'll see," Louie replied.

I led the way out the trail into the dark virgin forest. The deputies and Chief were right behind. Now we began hiking uphill as the path followed a ridgeline straight northwest. This was indeed Tornow country. I walked slowly, held my rifle at the ready, and carefully watched ahead through the trees and tangled thickets of salal, huckleberry and sword ferns. Each nerve and sensory system in my body was on full alert. The slightest movement caught my eye. From time to time the sun broke through the forest canopy high above us, streaming shafts of radiance onto the dense underbrush. I flinched in alarm when a small, gray chipmunk skittered up a windfall tree, scolding us for disturbing his morning nap.

"Can't we speed it up?" Charley asked.

I didn't answer but increased the pace a little. Faster meant careless and that worried me. There came a crashing in the brush ahead of us. I drew the hammer back on my rifle, eyes desperately searching for the cause of the noise.

Beside me, ears erect, Chief tested the air for a whiff of an intruder. "Did you fellas hear that?" I asked.

"Yeah," Louie replied, "probably an animal." I thought to myself, We're gettin' awful jittery over nothin'. If that was Tornow, we'd never hear that much noise, not with his uncanny skill at moving through the woods without a sound. Within a few seconds, a large cow elk with a tiny, spotted calf at her side appeared in an open spot in the brush. She turned and looked at us, curious if we were a threat to her baby. I heaved another sigh of relief. After several hours, the terrain levelled off and we came to a heavily timbered plateau. Perched on the limb of a slender vine maple nearby, a belted kingfisher rattled his cry of warning like a self-appointed sentry at our approach.

"We must be gettin' close to the lake," Louie whispered. "Them birds usually don't wander far from water."

In another hundred yards I held up my hand as a signal to stop. "Listen," I said. "Do you hear 'em?"

From just ahead came a caterwauling chorus of croaking frogs.

"I hear 'em," Charley said, "The lake can't be far now."

I dropped down on one knee and gathered the two deputies around me. "Listen, fellas, let's use our heads," I said in a low voice. "We'll just go a little farther and see if there's any sign of Tornow around here. Then we'll go back to the shack."

By the looks on their faces, I could tell they didn't agree with me, but they said nothing.

Ever so slowly, we picked our way across the soft swampy bog, careful not to step on anything that would make a noise. I clutched the battered, wooden stock of my Winchester, ready to shoot on reflex.

Suddenly, through the trees I spotted patches of open water, this had to be what we were looking for—the lake was just a short distance ahead. Within a few yards we came to the lakeshore and the trail wound across an unstable marsh dotted with asparagus-like shoots of common horsetail plants.

I was now crouched down low to hide my silhouette. It was quiet. Deathly quiet. I think we all three saw it at the same time.

"Look," Charley whispered, "smoke." A thin wisp of bluish wood smoke spiraled up out of the forest of evergreen trees blanketing the small island.

"He's there, let's go get him!" Louie exclaimed.

"No," I hissed anxiously, "don't do it."

The two deputies pushed past me towards the island on a short, wet trail carpeted with yellowish-green bog moss. Chief followed them.

"Get down." Already they were prime targets.

"You comin', Giles?" Charley whispered.

It was decision time for me. I felt the urge to turn back down the trail, follow the sheriff's orders. But I knew I wouldn't. I couldn't do it. Not this time.

Chapter Two

TWENTY-THREE YEARS EARLIER, IN A PRIMITIVE LOG CABIN ON the Tornow homestead, nine year-old John lay on a straw mattress in the sleeping loft, burning up with a life-threatening fever.

"It's the black measles doin' it," the venerable country doctor told Fritz and Louisa, John's parents, after he'd been attending to the youngster for two days. "If we can't break the fever, we may lose him. I've only known one person who survived a fever this high. And he was never the same afterwards."

"He'll pull through, I just know he will," Louisa said, her heavy German accent inflecting each word. "We have prayed very much for him," the stockily-built, fifty-two year old mother wiped her tears with a lacy, linen hankie.

Sitting beside her on the rough-hewn bench he'd chiseled from a cedar log, Fritz extended his heavily-calloused farmer's hand down to his wife's aproned lap. He gently curled his strong fingers around Louisa's wrinkled hand to emphasize his reassurance. "There, there, Mama, don't cry. Johnny will get better. Wait and see. The Lord will answer our prayers."

Across the home-built wooden table, Minnie Bauer, the oldest Tornow offspring was silhouetted by a coal-oil lamp. She, too, agonized over the doctor's prognosis. Minnie had spent several days away from her husband on their nearby homestead to help her mother nurse her favorite brother. She had married cantankerous old Henry Bauer in 1885 when she was eighteen. Her two daughters, Mary, three-and-a-half, and Lizzie, two, were staying at the crowded Tornow cabin with Minnie. Some said the reason she married Henry was because the Bauer place was handy, only a couple miles away, easy walking distance. Besides, both families immigrated from Germany and had known each other before they fled their native country around 1870 to avoid political oppression.

"I'll go upstairs and put another cold cloth on brother's forehead." Minnie got up from the dour gathering and swished her floor-length mother Hubbard around the bench. The attractive young woman with raven-black curls rolling down her back quickly strode to the water bucket in the corner.

"Thank you, Minnie," Louisa said, "I don't know how I'd manage without your help."

The youngest Tornow, seven year-old Edward, amused himself on the floor with a spool and string beside the rock fireplace in the small cabin.

Fearing for his son's life, Fritz allowed his mind to wander back to the early days. He and other German friends had immigrated to this promised land where acreage was free for homesteaders willing to work. Their glowing letters had lured him and other countrymen to this remote wilderness of Washington, which became a state in 1889. They came much like the pioneers across the prairie. Instead of coming overland they had travelled greater distances across the ocean to a new land, a new beginning. Life had been difficult for Fritz and Louisa. They had managed to scratch out a bare existence from their timbered uplands and brushy river-bottoms, mostly with bare hands and manual tools. But the Lord had been good to them. Although they'd lost two children as infants, five boys and Minnie had survived. Now Fritz prayed the Savior would again smile benevolently on his family and bring his son back from the edge of darkness.

Coming down the ladder-like stairway, Minnie told her mother,

"I put another wet cloth on Johnny's forehead, Ma. He's in a deep sleep and doesn't talk to me."

"I'd best go up and take a look," the doctor said, squinting his steely-grey eyes in thought. "We've got to break that fever. Maybe I'll give him some powders and see if that helps any."

As the doctor left, young Edward tried to climb into his mother's lap. "Will Johnny git better so we can go hunt rabbits?" the seven year-old asked, searching his mother's face for the answer.

"Don't fret, he'll soon be on the mend," Louisa replied with a pretended optimistic tone in her voice. Edward plopped into his mother's lap and rested his towhead against her pillowy breasts. He knew that was always rewarded with a hug and a kiss. That's what he needed now. "You're underfoot, Edward," she scolded him, "we're thinkin' real hard about your brother right now. I can't be bothered with you."

She brusquely lifted him down to the floor. The youngster was devastated. He began to cry big crocodile tears that rolled down his chubby little cheeks like raindrops on a window. Unhappy thoughts churned through his young head. Are they so busy jawin' about Johnny they ain't got no lovin' for me? For the first time in his young life he felt left out in the cold. Even crying didn't help. They just ignored him.

Soon the rough-sawed, wooden door opened. The other three Tornow boys, William, 17, Albert, 14 and Frederick, 12, wearily shuffled into the small cabin. Husky lads, they mirrored their father's six-foot, two-hundred pound frame. "We got those two stumps out, Pa," William said, tossing his wet raincoat on the floor near the fireplace. "Had to hitch up the horse to yank out all the roots."

"Good for you, come spring we'll level off that field and plant rutabagas."

"How's Johnny?" Albert asked, his eyes reflecting his deep concern.

"Not much change," Minnie replied. "The doctor's up there with him now. Says it could go either way."

The dire possibility of losing John cast a quiet pall over those seated around the common room. The single glass lamp sent beams of orange light dancing on the coarse sawed log walls. One small south-facing window was neatly framed by crisp, white lace curtains. In the midst of sparsity the curtains seemed out of place. Two antique, dark-wood picture frames hung on opposing walls like two elongated eyeballs staring at each other. In all likelihood, they were pictures of Fritz or Louisa's parents.

The doctor had tried every cure in his limited bag of medical tricks to quell John's high temperature. He'd even invented some new ones. Grass-roots experimental medicine, more or less. Over and over in his mind, he recalled the few simple procedures for reducing fevers. He'd overlooked nothing. At least nothing known to emerging medical science in the countrified 1890's.

Bending over his young patient, the doctor took the boy's temperature one more time that afternoon. All of a sudden John's eyes opened and he looked squarely into the physician's face as he uttered two beautiful words, "I'm hungry." The doctor felt John's somewhat cooler forehead, gave him a reassuring pat and smiled as he checked the thermometer.

"Land's sake, son, we'll get you something to eat right away." The physician hurried to spread the wonderful news, almost tripping down the steep stairs. "Johnny's awake and wants something to eat. The fever has broken," he shouted to the family.

Louisa momentarily bowed her head in prayer, "Thank You, dear Lord, and please bless our special doctor who brought Johnny from death's door."

"Go on with you," the physician replied, with a relieved grin.

First tiny cabin built by German immigrant, Henry Bauer, around the time of his marriage to Minnie Tornow.

"Your prayers are what pulled Johnny through."

Hearing the good news, Fritz and the boys rattled the log walls with their shouts and cheers of jubilation. They were celebrating a great victory.

Upstairs John heard the ruckus. A faint smile crossed his emaciated face. A smile like a beam of sunshine peeking through a chink in the log walls. Louisa hurriedly warmed a pot of chicken broth and weak tea over the glowing coals in the stone hearth.

When it was ready, Fritz carried the thin food up to his son. Before ascending the steep stairs, he wiped a tear from his dark eyes on the sleeve of his red flannel shirt.

"Must be a lot of gol-darn dust in here," he grumbled. The entire family went upstairs to see John.

But off in a corner of the downstairs cabin, withdrawn from all the celebration, hunched a small forlorn figure. He was hiding in his private little cranny. Edward, the forgotten child, crouched in the corner. The bedroom was so small the family and doctor could hardly squeeze in around John's narrow bunk.

"Good grief, what's all the fuss about?" the lad hoarsely whispered. His mother planted a big kiss on his forehead. "We all love you and we're tickled to death that you're feelin' better."

She began spooning the warm broth into her son's mouth. "Next, I want you to drink this tea. It will put roses back in your cheeks," she ordered in her imperious, parental tone of voice.

The doctor drew Fritz aside. Crooking thumbs into his two vest pockets, he whispered, "We're very fortunate that Johnny has survived this terrible fever, but I'll be surprised if it doesn't leave him with some kind of mental or physical infirmity. Only time will tell," he concluded.

"We're just glad to have him back," Fritz replied, a look of appreciation spreading across his large, bearded face. "We'll worry about those other things later. Many thanks for all you've done, we're surely grateful."

John suddenly raised up on one elbow. "Where's Edward?" he asked in a frail voice.

Then Fritz noticed his youngest son was missing. He went halfway down the stairs. He looked around the common room. Edward had disappeared.

Out in the barn, the youngster kicked absentmindedly at an old shovel propped up against the manger. Edward had a heavy heart. His world of reassured affection cradled by the warmth of his mother's bosom was shattered. They're all fussin' over Johnny and nobody cares 'bout me anymore, he thought to himself. Thinking these bad thoughts was a new feeling that swept over his juvenile psyche. In all of his nearly eight years of age, he'd never felt like this before. He had pangs of guilt about this new sense of self. Edward didn't recognize the flame of jealousy that kindled resentment in his young mind.

By late that afternoon, John was regaining his strength and sitting up in bed. He knew he'd been sick for awhile, but the youngster never realized he'd had a close brush with death at such an early age.

With the crisis over, Minnie told her folks, "I've gotta git home. Henry's probably fussin' over me bein' gone for such a spell. Besides, the girls need to git back to their own beds."

William hitched the team to the buggy as Minnie and her two girls climbed in back. It had been raining but now the gray clouds churned towards the mountains. An early-spring sun barely lightened the muddy lane out of the small farm. Cocoa-colored mud puddles dotted the road which was really nothing more than a wagon-width trail cut through the homestead's stump-littered pasture.

As the pair of draft horses plodded the narrow byway, tall tansy heads, growing between the wheel ruts, scraped and rattled on the bottom of the buggy. William drew a deep breath, relishing the pleasurable aroma of air cleansed by spring showers and tinged by the fragrance of nearby early-blossoming Pacific crab apple trees.

It was an easy twenty-minute drive to the Bauer homestead. William reined the team into the front yard. Henry had built the little cabin alone from lumber sawed from trees felled on the 160–acre Satsop valley spread.

He'd heard them coming. The German father stood in the doorway in his faded blue bib overalls, defiant hands on hips as if to deny entry. "So at last you decided to come home to roost," he commented with sarcasm in his deep guttural accent as Minnie and the girls approached the cabin.

Without looking at her husband, Minnie said, "I been helpin' Ma while Johnny was sick." She brushed past him.

"That don't cut no ice with me," he spit out in anger. "Seems to me they got a passle of help over there with all them young 'uns. You got chores to do here, you know. Did you forget about your home?"

William scooped up his sister's belongings in his arms but hesitated as he headed for the Bauer cabin. He was afraid of his Uncle Henry, especially when he was in a vile mood. William briefly thought about leaving the baggage and running, but decided not to.

Henry stopped him at the door, his face twisted into an angry scowl. "Ain't no need for you to come in, gimme her stuff and you can leave."

"I was just tryin' to help her, Uncle Henry."

"Best way you can help is to stay gone," the Bauer elder snapped at him. "And tell your kinfolk not to butt in. She belongs here and that's that."

William slapped the team with the reins to circle out of the Bauer yard. Henry stomped up the porch, went inside and slammed the door, venting his anger.

During the short drive home, William realized that his uncle's tirade had scared him and left him with an empty, uncomfortable feeling. He wondered why he acted that way, so crotchety, and mean to his own family. The youngster remembered that Pa had told him it was because Henry was jealous of the time Minnie spent with her folks. Time that Henry couldn't control.

In just a few days John had recuperated from his near lethal bout with the measles and resultant fever. He went outside for the first time. Although it was a cold spring day, he basked in the brisk mountain air, invigorated by the essence of lofty evergreens wafting down from the nearby forest. He even enjoyed the pungent aroma of the barnyard. John was just happy to be alive, to be outdoors, to feel vibrant and energetic again. Eagerness surrounded him like a litter of new pups chasing their own tails. He had heard his parents and the doctor talking about his illness and what might happen to him after the fever. He had asked Ma what "infirmity" meant. As a test of himself, quick as a flash he jumped up and straddled the split-rail fence around the pasture. Everything seemed to work O.K. He shook his arms and legs, nothing wrong with them. He tested his eyes, listened to faint sounds, even stuck out his tongue at the brown draft horse that was staring intently at him. He didn't seem to have any of them infirmities. Leastways none he could locate.

Within a week or so, John was able to return to the tiny, one-room schoolhouse just down the road from the Tornow home place. The teacher and all the kids welcomed him back. But as days faded into weeks, he noticed that school was not as much fun as it once was. He began to isolate himself from the others. He worked alone, played alone, felt more comfortable when others weren't around him.

This developing trait was soon noticed by John's parents. "Have you seen how Johnny doesn't join in much with the other boys of late?" Louisa asked her husband one day, working the handle on the well-worn butter churn.

"Yes, he's becoming somewhat of a loner," Fritz replied, cogitating as he filled his pipe with shreds of dark brown tobacco from a leather pouch. "Maybe I should get to know him better, spend some time alone with him. Hate to be gone from the farm but it might be a good idea if just the two of us went off into the woods for a few days."

"Go easy with him, he's my own special son after all he's been through," Louisa replied, peering into the churn's innards.

It was a bright summer day when Fritz and John packed their blankets and a few provisions into canvas satchels and headed into the thick forest north of the farm. Ever since his father had suggested they go traipsin' and campin', John eagerly anticipated their day of departure like he looked forward to Christmas. He enjoyed the outdoors, his favorite place to be.

They followed the path towards the river. Fritz carried his rifle. He too enjoyed the outdoors and wished he had time to get out more often. The pair skirted the pasture, edged with showy spreads of bright-yellow creeping buttercup, the farmer's curse.

Before they entered the dense timber, father and son turned and waved goodbye to the mother standing in the cabin's doorway. Oh I hope they're careful, she fretted, nervously twisting her hankie in her long, bony fingers.

Through dried tears on his young face, someone else dejectedly saw the pair disappear into the forest. Edward watched them leave from a window in the loft. He wanted to go too.

It was a rewarding trek for both of them. They camped out in the rugged, timbered country for almost a week, exhilarated by the vibrant and dynamic pulse of the remote wilderness. Father and son tramped wide game trails that had been cut into the forest floor by deer and elk for many decades. They meandered their way deeper and deeper into the majestic Olympic Mountains and Fritz shared his considerable outdoor knowledge with John. "This here's a coyote track. See how it's long and skinny. Bobcat tracks are bigger and rounder." They mostly lived off the land.

The Tornow father intended this experience to provide outdoorsman lore for John while, at the same time, bonding the father-son relationship. He thought perhaps it would help the youngster develop a more comfortable feeling with his father and with others. John was an enthusiastic pupil, eager to learn more about his beloved wilderness.

One day Fritz led his son to a stagnant pool of water backed up from a slow-running stream. "If you ever git lost and real hungry, this is the best soup you kin eat." He scooped up a cupful of the thick, green gunk from the top of the putrid pool. "Just build a fire and boil this stuff, then drink it. It's chock full of healthy things that will keep you alive for days."

"Aaag," John rumbled deep within his throat, "that stuff looks terrible, Pa. Who could eat it?"

"Just remember what I tell you. This is one way to keep alive in the woods if you run out of grub."

As a hairy marmot eyed the intruders with suspicion from his elevated mound, Fritz taught John how to drop a string noose from a long stick over the head of an unsuspecting grouse. Later, a short line and hook baited with red huckleberries produced all the fish they could eat from a mountain stream.

One day they surprised an elk herd on it's way to higher summer pastures, having wintered in the temperate lowlands. Fritz and John sneaked through the timber to get closer to the animals without spooking them. Crouched low, father and son quietly positioned themselves behind a huge Douglas fir blowdown.

They watched the animals browse on dwarf blueberry brush and tender deciduous vine maple stems. "There must be fifty, maybe sixty elk in the herd," Fritz whispered.

"Look at that big five-point bull standin' broadside to us. You gonna shoot?" John asked.

"We ain't got no use for all the meat on one of those big critters this trip, so we won't kill one," Fritz said. "The good Lord put them here for us to use wisely. Always remember; waste not, want not."

But they did some shooting. An alpine meadow above timberline was adorned with a bevy of nature's colorful ornamentals. The landscape was alive with the large, orange-flowered tiger lilies, their purple-spotted heads nodding in the mountain breeze. Tall stalks of bear grass displayed prolific clusters of tiny, white blossoms.

The German father took his knife from it's belt sheath. He cut a white mark on the base of a stunted mountain fir tree. Next, they backed off a couple hundred yards. Handing John the rifle, Fritz said, "There she be, let me see you put one right in the middle of that white spot."

This wasn't the first time John had shot. He knew about rifles.

He thought to himself, this will be an easy one. I'll show Pa how good I am. He threw the gun to his shoulder and cranked off a shot, then jacked another cartridge into the chamber and shot again, just like a veteran.

With eager anticipation they walked up and inspected the tree. "Not bad," Fritz smiled. "About an inch low, second one's a bit high, both in the target. Now come back here, I want to show you somethin'."

Pacing off just a hundred yards Fritz told his son, "This time I want you to forget you've got sights on the barrel. Try to shoot without sighting. Just throw the rifle to your shoulder and shoot by instinct. Learn to sense the bullet to the target."

The father and son were miles from the closest inhabitants. There was no one around on that afternoon to hear the rifle shots time and again echoing off the tall peaks of the Olympics as Fritz taught his son to shoot by instinct—without sighting. The lad was thrilled to learn this new method of shooting. Fritz put a muscular arm around his son's shoulders to show his satisfaction with John's performance. But he might not have been so satisfied if he could have forseen where guns in the future might lead his son.

Following a hearty supper of plump trout and golden potatoes baked to perfection over the campfire coals, they sat around talking long past bedtime. They were camped in a grove of spruce and cedar giants where the first limbs were fifty feet off the ground. Above them in the darkness, barely discernible in the fading campfire glow, a spotted owl, like a wise old forest sentinel, watched them closely from its high perch on a stubby spruce branch. Leaning against the base of a huge cedar, Fritz slowly tamped tobacco into his crusty, blackened pipe.

"How you been feelin' lately, son?" he asked, an inquisitive look in his eyes. "Just fair to middlin', Pa," the boy said, licking up the last

remaining crumbs of baked trout with his fingers.

"Seems I'm better than I was before the fever, at least in most places. Thing that bothers me though is I get all jangly when I'm around people. Oh, I don't mean you or Ma, but others. Makes me feel funny in the head, like the world is closin' in on me. Ain't easy to explain about it."

"I wouldn't worry none, that'll probably go away in time. Mark my words and make no bones about it."

"I hope so. Don't like that feelin' I get in my noggin'."

Neither Fritz nor John, probably not even the medicos of the late 1800's would have recognized the youngster's behavior as the early stages of a sociological disorder, which would get worse. Much worse.

On their last day in the forest, Fritz prepared a breakfast of johnny-cake and fried the last of their bacon slab. The pair doused their campfire and started for home under a scattered buttermilk sky. A gentle breeze glided through the lofty tops of the towering evergreen forest monarchs. To John Tornow, it sounded like a murmuring forest lullaby. It would one day evolve into a beckoning wilderness call that would seductively lure him back to an environment that would become his evil mistress. A mistress from whom he could not escape.

On the return hike father and son traversed an aromatic grove of young Pacific silver firs interspersed with western yew, prized by native inhabitants for bow-making.

Louisa heard the horses in the pasture whinny a greeting to Fritz and John as they hiked out of the timber. Peeling spuds, she wiped her hands on her flour sack apron before rushing out to meet them. She was so happy they were home at last.

Around the huge wooden table that evening after everyone had gone to bed, Fritz and Louisa talked about family things. "While you was away Minnie visited one day but left in a hurry because she said

Henry's been givin' her a bad time. He says she's gotta stay home or he'll make her wish she had. That ol' sod scares the daylights outta her."

Fritz pondered that news before angrily replying, "He's just a damned ass." Louisa drew a sharp breath. She was unaccustomed to hearing her husband use swear words. But she understood his anger that someone would mistreat his only daughter, his second love.

* * *

During the 1890's the crossroads community around Matlock near the Tornow homestead was beginning to see the influx of several logging companies. They sought the abundant timber stands that blanketed the higher foothills.

William Tornow, now just short of his twentieth birthday, hesitantly sat down to talk with his patriarch father late one summer evening. "Pa, I'd really like to go get a job loggin' if it's alright with you. I can make a dollar-fifty a day buckin' (sawing) downed trees for Port Blakely and they only charge fifty-cents a day room and board."

Fritz replied, "Ain't no use we hem and haw about this. If you're really dead set on leavin', guess you should pack your bindle and do 'er. You'll find it ain't no picnic out there, but you gotta live and learn on your own. For that kind of money they'll work your tail off. But you can handle it."

Fritz and Louisa hated to see their oldest son leave the nest, but took it in their stride. "Can't keep 'em home forever," Fritz said, thumbing through the Farmer's Almanac he'd borrowed from the storekeeper.

Being the youngest, Edward thought he should be given special favors by his parents, especially his mother. But following John's recuperation, Louisa seemed to heap most of her love and affection on John. She called him, "Her special child." Edward was often neglected. He noticed this and it didn't help quell his burning fire of jealousy. Not a bit.

While John and Edward both found plenty of childhood mischief to get into, they seldom collaborated. Each had his own special brand of devilment.

* * *

One evening during mid-summer the fragrant scent of apple blossoms from the bottomland orchard floated on a soft breeze. A full moon nearly transformed night into day. A young figure moved furtively towards a window in the Tornow's upstairs sleeping loft. A dry floor board creaked sharply. The youngster froze in midstep. Had anyone heard? Relieved that he'd been undetected, the boy moved to the open window and stepped out onto the ladder reaching to the ground. Circling around to the path, he was surprised that only a few shafts of yellow moonlight filtered through the treetops in the timber. It was dark under the trees. Suddenly he was startled by a strange whumping noise in the blackness. The youngster broke out in tiny droplets of cold sweat, unaccustomed to strange things that thumped in the night. It was scary. In a few moments he breathed a sigh of relief as he saw the outline of a large barn owl noisily clumping it's massive wings from tree to tree in search of prey.

Walking fast, almost running through the timber, he spotted his destination within a half-hour—the Bauer chicken house. He thought of the potential risks involved with his plan. He could turn back. Go home. But he wouldn't change his mind tonight. He wanted to do this. He'd show 'em. The youngster quietly opened the door and stepped inside to the pungent odor of oozy chicken manure. The flock of leghorns squatted on their perch like a row of targets at a shooting gallery. A couple of hens eyed him with suspicion but didn't move away from him, although one softly clucked with a tone of apprehension. How to do this without making noise, he pondered. He reached for the neck of the closest hen. She saw his threatening hand approach, eyed it with uncertainty, but didn't back away. A fatal decision. A quick twist and he dropped the warm, lifeless bird into his gunny sack.

The remainder of the flock became uneasy at this sudden action. The clucking sounds intensified. He missed a second grab when the intended victim noisily flapped her wings and flew to the floor. He moved down the perch; number three flew out of reach; likewise number four. Now he moved faster down the line and caught the next hen in her indecision but he didn't get a firm grip on her neck. During her few remaining moments of life, she literally squawked her head off. By now, pandemonium broke loose in the chicken house. Feathers flew and a dozen beating wings raised a cloud of dust from the straw-covered floor as the cacophony from the frantic chickens beat against his young eardrums.

He wanted out. Now. Tightly clutching his gunny sack, the boy beat a hasty retreat out of the yard and into the woods. Glancing over his shoulder, his fear mounted as he saw the unmistakable yellow lantern glow in the cabin's window.

Uncle Henry had heard the ruckus and was coming to investigate. The lad was frightened, really frightened. In fact, he was scared to death. Missing the trail in the dark, he ran like a terrified deer through the forest, gasping for breath, fear blazing in his eyes. In ten or fifteen minutes he arrived at the secret hideout. He crawled into the small opening of the cave and laid back in the dry dirt. He was hidden from any pursuer, from meddlesome people, from those who didn't understand him. Now he was completely shielded. This was his childlike haven of tranquility, his own secure castle, complete with imaginary moats and dragons. He even had guardian knights who brandished slashing swords. Safe at last. In a while, the lad plucked and cleaned the two chickens with his knife, just like Ma had taught him. Next he washed them in a nearby tiny creek and picked a cool spot in the back of the cave to hang the chickens. They'd be safe there.

At home the next day he asked his brother, "How about we go stay tonight at the cave?" John and Edward had discovered the hideout earlier while they were searching for berries. They considered it to be their own special hideaway.

Louisa approved the overnight jaunt. "Now you two be careful out there. I'd best fix you some grub to take along."

"We won't need much, Ma." They packed utensils and a few provisions into their satchels, grabbed an old blanket and soon skittered down the trail towards the cave. As John trudged along the path with his brother on that mild afternoon he thought to himself, I'm sure glad Edward is acting more friendly with me lately. Hope he's over his mad.

The youngsters dipped a tin cup of cool water from the burbling little stream laced with white-flowered, water buttercups.

Afterwards, they plopped down to rest at the cave's entrance. John looked out at the tall, red alders in the river-bottom, the rolling green hills overgrown with triple- petalled, western trilliums and

The Bauer family moved into this larger home shortly after 1900. Both houses are located just off the West Boundary road and are owned by Hap Hollatz.

yellow-flowered Oregon ash. John asked Edward, "Don't you just love this place?" They had unloaded their satchels in the deeper environs of the hideout when the Tornow youngster spied the two chickens, white and denuded, hanging in a dark corner. "Where'd the chickens come from?"

His brother replied, "They're for supper tonight. They's not chickens, just big grouse."

"You can't pull the wool over my eyes, I knows chickens when I sees 'em," his brother argued.

"Don't look a gift horse in the mouth. Just think how good they'll cook up for supper tonight."

Later that afternoon they built a fire in front of the cave. John asked, "Shall we roast the birds over the fire on a willow spit like Pa taught me?"

"Suits me," Edward replied, throwing a dry piece of an alder limb on the crackling fire. After the brothers polished off the two birds and a loaf of Ma Tornow's fresh bread for supper, they relaxed in front of the cave, warmed by the fire's red glow.

"Did you kill two of Ma's chickens?"

"No."

"Then where did you say they come from?"

"I didn't." It was obvious he wasn't going to get any more information from his brother about the two birds.

When the boys awoke the next morning, it was like they hadn't eaten in days.

"My backbone is rubbin' against my belly button," John exclaimed.

"Maybe if we hurry we can git back in time for noon dinner," Edward suggested. They quickly beat it for home.

Fritz had been at the mill selling a load of logs off the lower-forty. Now he hurried home so he could join the family in the noontime meal. Reining up in front of the tiny log cabin, he didn't even take time to unharness Darby and Daisy. Instead he reached into a box beneath the spring seat and carried a tiny four-legged bundle inside. He was surprised to see John and Edward home so soon.

"Did the bears chase you two out of the woods?" he asked with a faint smile that barely turned up the corners of his mouth above his bushy beard.

"No, Pa, we got hungry," Edward said.

"Come here, John, I got something for you." As John approached, his father pulled a brown puppy out of an oversize pocket in his gray mackinaw. "Harry's bitch hound at the mill had six pups. He gave me this little fellow for you."

John's eyes lit up like sparklers on the Fourth of July. "For me, Pa? Really for me?"

Fritz said, "He's all yours but you gotta take care of him. Make sure he gets food and water every day."

"I will, I promise. He's the cutest little feller I've ever saw. What should I name him?" the youngster asked, clutching the tiny bundle of fur to his chest.

Louisa looked disdainfully at the pup. "He can stay inside awhile, but soon's he's big enough, out he goes. Trouble with cute pups, soon they grow up to be dawgs," she said, ladling the venison stew into each bowl on the table. Dogs didn't impress Mother Tornow.

After a few minutes deliberation John said, "Cougar, that's what I'll call him. Cougar. I'll bet his ma and pa caught lots of cougars." The new master fixed a bed in a corner of the cabin, putting a ragged gunny sack into a small wooden box. Cougar promptly hopped in and fell fast asleep.

Edward slid off his bench at the table, walked over to Fritz and tugged at his shirt sleeve. "What did you bring me, Pa?" he whimpered, rubbing his runny nose against his father's shirt.

"Why son, I didn't bring you nothin'. You'll have to wait for Christmas," Fritz said as he speared another chunk of venison out of the stew bowl.

John spent the day with his new friend, carrying him around in his arms, introducing the pup to the farm animals, and defending Cougar from Ma.

During their late evening talk, the Tornow parents agreed that John's attitude had mellowed with the pup's arrival. "Seems to have brought him out of his shell somewhat," Fritz said, "so you be good to that dog."

"Yes, you're right," Louisa replied as she clicked her knitting needles in front of the stone hearth, "but soon's it gets big enough, it's still goin' outside. There's enough bodies in this cabin already, we don't need no more."

* * *

Henry Bauer argued with himself as he sat at the kitchen table the next afternoon. He really didn't want to go to the Tornows but knew he must. The reluctant homesteader needed to clear up the mystery of who'd stolen his chickens. He had a hunch one of the Tornow boys might know something about the thievery.

Pulling on his jacket, he told Minnie, "I'm gonna go over to Tornows and see what I can learn about my missin' hens."

"Let me take the girls and go with you. Ma ain't seen the kids for better'n a month." How time had flown, Mary was four, Lizzie was two. A couple of the cutest little girls in the valley.

Minnie bundled up the kids while Henry harnessed the team to the wagon. At the sound of the horses plodding up the drive, Louisa looked out the curtained window as she was shelling peas for supper. "Land sakes, here comes the Bauers, the whole kit 'n' kaboodle of 'em, even Henry."

Fritz couldn't believe what his wife was seeing. He got up from his battered old wooden rocker and joined her peering out the window.

"Well, I'll be jiggered, wonder what he wants?" Louisa met them at the door, embraced Minnie with a warm hug, then each of the girls in turn.

She stiffly shook hands with Henry, "Won't you please come in?" Fritz solemnly greeted Henry. Neither wasted words, a simple handshake with poker-faces, "Henry," and "Fritz." There wasn't room in the tight little cabin for everyone to sit so most just stood.

Getting right to the point, Henry said, "I don't mean to come bargin' in here like this but I had a problem in my hen house the other night."

The young Tornow brother hung his head, staring at the floor.

"What's your hen house got to do with us?" Fritz asked defiantly, the muscles in his jaw tightening. "Lost two hens, I did. It warn't varmints, 'cause the door hasp had been opened. I seen the thief runnin' away but couldn't make him out in the dark. Just wanted to ask if your boys might know anythin' 'bout it," the elder Bauer concluded, staring straight ahead at a blank log wall. Fritz stiffened to his full six-feet, maybe an inch or two more, his fists doubled until the knuckles turned white.

"Now just hold on there a minute, Henry. I don't think my boys had nothin' to do with your missin' hens."

John and Edward stood in silence, heads down, staring at the rough-sawed plank floor. John waited for his brother to say something, to admit his wrong-doings or at least his involvement in the chicken incident. After an embarrassing long silence, John raised his head, looked his father straight in the eyes, and said, "I took 'em Pa. I stole Uncle Henry's chickens, then me and Edward roasted and ate 'em at our hideout down at the creek."

Edward continued to hang his head, saying nothing, but now a slight impish smile crossed his boyish face.

Fritz Tornow stood like a pillar of stone. Louisa was dumbstruck, staring at John with unbelieving eyes. The silence lingered in the room like a heavy, iron blanket for what seemed an eternity.

Fritz said, "It would appear you are right and my boys have been up to no good. I aim to find out more about this and they'll face the music." From the crushed look on the patriarch's face, it appeared he had died a thousand deaths

"Sorry it had to come to this, Fritz," Henry said, his Teutonic features now softening a bit. In a low, ominous voice the father demanded, "John, Edward, I want both of you upstairs right this minute."

"We didn't mean no harm, Pa," John cried. "Upstairs, I said." A little louder this time.

Heads hanging, both boys climbed the stairs to the loft. Louisa finally spoke, "This is a terrible shock. They're usually good boys."

"Just playin' a little tomfoolery," Minnie shrugged, trying to lighten the mood of the tense atmosphere. "

"Ain't no excuse," Fritz countered in his usual strident tone, "I don't take no likin' to this kind of goin's on."

The staunch father went to the cupboard where Louisa kept her butter and egg money. "Here's three dollars, that should be enough to square us for the hens," he said in a subdued voice, handing the money to Henry.

"More than enough. I don't like takin' it from you."

"Fair is fair," Fritz replied.

"Well, we best be gettin' along," Henry said to Minnie, turning awkwardly towards the door. "Sorry to have caused you this aggravation."

"We're shameful it happened," Fritz said, shaking hands with reluctance, looking at Henry straight on. Louisa's eyes glistened with

unfallen tears, hugging her daughter and granddaughters as they went out the door.

The Bauers piled into the wagon and pulled out of the yard. Driving onto the rutted, dirt road, Henry felt good about the moral victory over his perennial nemesis. Within himself, he gloated. He'd humbled Fritz Tornow. And as he smiled, he thought, Tornow might have a better farm, bigger family, more livestock, and a few more dollars in the bank; but by God he'd brought him down a peg or two this time.

As they sat on their upstairs bunks, Edward asked John, "Why'd you 'fess up to it?"

"I'm the oldest and when you didn't speak your piece I just figgered it was my place to tell about it."

Then a look of fear clouded the faces of the two youngsters. Footsteps on the stairs. Pa was coming. The elder Tornow stood straight, tall and solemn in the middle of the loft, the only place in the cramped room where the pitch of the roof allowed him to stand upright. To the boys he represented the judge, jury and executioner. Staring at them with a look that would crush granite, he spoke slowly and very deliberate.

"I need to have it out with you two. John, why did you steal them chickens?"

"Just fer fun, Pa, didn't mean nothin' by it," John cried.

"I should take my belt to the both of you," Fritz declared, his darkened face twisted in a threatening scowl like a smoldering volcano ready to erupt. "If ever I catch either of you pulling a low-down stunt like this again, I'll tan your britches from here to Sunday. I want no more monkey shines."

As he came downstairs, Fritz had that hard look in his eyes, and was shaking his head like he couldn't believe what he'd just heard.

Louisa sat alone at the table staring blankly at her clenched

Bauer twins, John and William, posed on front porch of their home. Picture was taken shortly before their murders, which were blamed on John Tornow.

hands resting on her clean, white apron. She knew how devastating this confession of guilt was to her husband. She worried about the consequences.

"I can't believe my own boys would do such a thing," Fritz said. "And now, neither of them seems sorry for what they've done."

"Little Johnny couldn't steal anyone's chickens, Pa. But if you'd ask me, I don't believe Edward could neither."

"I'm not so sure John is the guilty one," Fritz said.

If the chicken theft actually happened, the truth was never revealed. The rift between the brothers seemed to deepen. Soon, John's withdrawal from other family members became more pronounced, and he felt betrayed. Cougar was John's only solace. Weeks later, sitting in a secluded spot overgrown with flowery shoots of slender whipplevine near the homestead, John would hold his now grown-up dog in his arms and tell Cougar about all his worries.

"Why do I feel like such an outcast from the family? Can you figger it out?"

The tawny hound would stare questioningly into John's face as if he was trying to help him find these difficult answers. Answers to questions that would haunt John for the rest of his life.

Chapter Three

HE SLAMMED THE SILVER-TIPPED CARTRIDGES INTO THE RIFLE'S well-oiled steel chamber on that gray and dreary afternoon during the spring of 1891. He always kept his rifle oiled and ready to use. Next he put six more bullets in his pocket. He stooped to pick one up that had dropped on the cabin's rough-hewn log floor. His fingers were slippery from handling the oily gun. He stepped outside under an overcast sky that lacked any promise of decent weather. Not soon anyway. That didn't matter.

The German homesteader was filled with frustration and bitterness over events of the past few months. But he knew what would ease his tension, make him feel better. The cold north wind blowing past the axe-carved porch pillars sent a shiver through his wiry frame. To combat the nippy breeze, he buttoned his well-worn, red-checkered mackinaw and pulled down his slouch hat. Standing on the front step, he looked around to make sure nobody was in sight, nobody to bother him, no witnesses. Out in the pasture a few head of scrawny livestock grazed on the quackgrass and alpine timothy that had found life on the forest floor after the surrounding trees had been harvested. Only stumps remained. It was time to do it. He picked out one of the larger stumps as his target, away from the livestock, out of danger. Darkening clouds swirled to the north as a pair of ravens played in flight, rolling and twisting at their game of airborne tag. He clutched the steel-gray rifle, cold and smooth to his touch. He walked to a small Sitka spruce sapling to rest the gun, to steady his aim, test his accuracy. The homesteader drew a careful bead, placing the rifle's front sight on the target stump two hundred yards away.

The hillside was covered with bleached-out tree remains, the nude by-product of logging. Why did he choose this one? Tall and broad at shoulder height, it was special. It reminded him of everyone who'd been unkind to him in this country after he had escaped political oppression in the fatherland. Henry Bauer pulled the trigger of his .45/70 calibre rifle and the sharp blast hammered his ear drums. This was the best way to vent his anger and frustration. The Bauer elder shot into the stump time after time. With each volley, he imagined the stump represented a different person, someone he wanted to punish; Fritz Tornow who had so much more than he had, a bigger family, a better farm, more livestock, a wife who stayed home and cared for his every need. He hated him. Hated him with a passion. Another volley hit the stump. There, take that!

Sometimes Henry felt serious pangs of guilt when he imagined the stump to be Minnie who seemed so calloused towards him; who spent so much time away from him; who really didn't seem to care anymore. Or the target could take on the likeness of many others; George, the money-grubbing storekeeper; the circuit riding mailman who pronounced his name "Bear;" the tax assessor who overvalued his property; or the young timber buyer, who'd ridden in with his fancy duds and shiny, brass-trimmed buggy a few weeks ago, made eyes at Minnie, and tried to buy his remaining timber for half it's value. The stump was unyielding. It absorbed the best Henry had to offer. But when the shooting was over, he felt much better. He felt vindicated.

At the same time on the Tornow place, Fritz hoofed it to the well for a cool drink. His muscular, tall frame and deliberate long stride made him look every bit like a western lawman. His wiry black beard, now graying in his forty-seventh year, took on the appearance of curly, black metal shavings often found on the floor of the local machine shop.

Fritz had been logging a patch of timber down by the river and grubbing out the pesky, yellow Scotch broom. In an instant, he stopped and listened. Shots. Sounded like they were coming from the mountains, towards the Bauer place. Wonder what that's all about, he thought to himself, then shrugged it off. Maybe just hunters.

* * *

During that summer John and Cougar spent many pleasurable days together roaming the woodlands near the homestead. They began staying out overnight, often at the hidden cave. The pair were inseparable. The youngster began harboring secret fears and experiencing sporadic spells of anxiety. Talking to Cougar proved to be John's most viable safety valve for relieving the pressure of these unfamiliar and disturbing visitations.

"We'll just stay in the cave where nobody can git to us or hurt us," John told his four-legged friend as they furtively crept through the forest toward the sanctuary. The dog hurried beside him as if he understood the need for haste in reaching the safety of their lair.

"Out here's where we belong," he told his floppy-eared listener. "Away from the family, away from Uncle Henry and all that fightin' and fussin' that goes on. Just you 'n me 'n the animals, peaceful and quiet-like."

One day while seated at the cave's entrance, John spotted a movement through the forest of alder trees that grew thick as porcupine quills in the bottomland. "Quiet, Cougar, someone's comin'," he whispered, placing a grimy hand on the dog's muscular neck.

Soon a man dressed in buckskin pants and jacket like a trapper or prospector appeared at quite a distance. He was just moseying through the red alders and black cottonwoods, packsack on his back and carrying an ancient-looking rifle.

"Let's see what this stranger is up to," John whispered to his dog, slipping out of the cave, crouching down low and dodging from tree to tree to keep from being seen. They stealthily followed the man for more than a mile, never getting close enough to be detected. The lad was practicing his tracking skills.

"He doesn't even know we're here," John whispered to Cougar. "If we was after him, we could sneak right up on him if we wanted."

The pair stayed with the cat and mouse game for a couple of hours, turning back when John was afraid he was getting into unknown territory. It was near suppertime, almost dark, when the boy and his dog returned home.

Louisa stopped them at the door like a gate tender. "You can come in, but that dawg stays out," she ordered. At the dinner table that evening, as he reached for another helping of rutabagas, John told the family, "Me and Cougar was followed out of the woods by a dangerous lookin' fella today."

Fritz looked up from carving a juicy beef roast. Casting a quizzical look of disbelief, he asked, "What'd he look like?" "I dunno, guess he was after me for somethin'. We was scared, but we got away."

Fritz and Louisa exchanged questioning glances but dismissed John's surprise announcement as simply a ploy for attention.

"It was maybe someone wantin' to spank you for bad things you done," Edward suggested, slopping more gravy on his mashed potatoes.

"Ain't done nothin'," John shot back, "he must have thought I was you by mistake."

Cozily curled in bed that night, in hushed tones the Tornow parents discussed John's story and its lack of detail.

"Seems strange there'd be somebody out in our woods," Fritz said. "Although I did hear some shots out there awhile back."

"Must have been just his imagination playin' tricks on him," Louisa said, snuggling warmly up to her husband.

"Yeah, maybe. But have you noticed he's talked more and more of late about things like that? Worries me a bit. Never anythin' for certain, but just a fear of folks watchin' him, or followin' him. Reminds me of what the Doc told us."

"Just a spell he's goin' through, he'll shuck it off when he gits a little older. Go to sleep Pa, and don't fret so much."

* * *

Henry Bauer's displeasure with the Tornows didn't keep his head-strong wife from once in awhile visiting her parents and brothers. "He can go to grass if he don't like it," she told her mother one balmy autumn day in 1891.

She was at the homestead to help her mother pick and preserve blueberries. They had almost finished pouring the hot, syrupy berries into Mason jars when a buggy with a lone driver pulled into the yard. "My, look at the pretty rig and that good-lookin' horseflesh," Louisa said. Minnie wiped her hands on a stained apron, leaned on her mother as they both peered out the cabin window scrutinizing the just-arrived visitor. "And the fella drivin' it ain't too bad neither," Minnie commented as the stranger stepped down from the shiny buggy painted blue and red with brass scrolls.

This comment brought a slight smile to Louisa's work-wrinkled face, but she also recognized it as improper coming from her married daughter. She chastised Minnie, "Shame on you, Daughter. You ain't supposed to be sizin' up men like that no more."

"I can if I want," Minnie shot back. "Besides, sometimes I don't feel like I've even got a husband the way he treats me." With a puzzled look, she continued, "I think this is the same fellow who stopped by our place and talked with Henry a few weeks ago. Don't remember much except he was sure good lookin'."

At twenty-four, Minnie Tornow Bauer had bloomed into radiant womanhood. She was an attractive young lady and two babies hadn't noticeably affected her voluptuous figure. Heads turned when she entered a room. Men's heads.

Stepping down from the fancy buggy, the dapper young man walked to the hitching rail with a lofty air of confidence. He tied his horse, a Morgan walker that looked almost as showy as the driver.

As he approached the cabin, Minnie noticed he was fashionably dressed in woodsy outdoor clothes; checkered flannel shirt, smooth-pressed, forest green whipcords and high-top leather boots so brand spankin' new and shiny, they looked like they'd never walked in dirt.

The two women stroked their hair back with both hands as they primped and smoothed tresses that had strayed. Minnie checked her face in a small broken mirror that hung by a string on the cabin wall. Louisa went to the door, Minnie almost in lockstep behind her.

"Good afternoon, ladies. I'm John Kennedy, timber buyer. I'm looking for Fritz Tornow."

"He's went to town," Louisa said with a neighborly smile. Minnie chimed in, all but climbing over her mother's back. "But he might be back soon, why don't you come in and wait?"

Mother Tornow was flabbergasted that Minnie would invite the stranger in. But she had to admit he was quite handsome and had a pleasing aroma about him, some kind of men's foo-faw. "Sit a spell," Minnie told the visitor as he entered the cabin, squinting his eyes to adjust to the dim light.

She pulled out a bench from the table while she shooed Mary and Lizzie to a bunk in the corner, like a mother hen chasing away her chicks. "I'll fix a pot of tea. Maybe you'd like to try a slice of home-made bread with some blueberry jam we just made," Minnie said, admiring the timber buyer's handsome features and elegant clothes.

Kennedy's eyes followed Minnie's every movement. Like a judge at a beauty pageant, he mentally visualized her young figure beneath the all-concealing dress.

"Why do you want to see Pa?" Mother Tornow asked.

Breaking his concentration on Minnie, he stammered, "Uhh… well…you see, the fellows at the sawmill told me that Mr. Tornow was bringing in a few logs to sell so I thought he might want to sell direct to me."

"You'll have to speak to him about that but I don't have a clue when he'll be home." She thought maybe he'd take the hint and leave. He didn't.

"Good golly that's the best jam I've ever had," the timber buyer exclaimed, wiping his chin with a napkin, after a second slice of fresh bread and a gulp of tea. "Where'd you pick the blueberries?"

"We got gobs of 'em down by the river," Minnie said staring into his handsome, clean-cut face. "Would you like to go pick some with me?"

Louisa coughed to catch her breath following Minnie's invitation, then stood up and walked towards the cabin door hoping the visitor would follow. "Mr. Kennedy probably has to run along, Daughter, I'll wager he's got logs to buy…somewhere…or other."

"Actually, no, I don't. I'd like to pick a few blueberries. It would also give me a chance to look at your stand of timber."

"Ma, can you look after the girls for me?"

"Well, yes, reckon I can do that." Minnie led Kennedy down the path towards the river on that warm October afternoon. But subconsciously she seemed not to be on the path, not at the Tornow cabin, instead she was in a wondrous fantasy fairyland with imaginary castles, pink clouds, a handsome prince, and not a care in the world.

Still holding her half-empty teacup, as if mesmerized, Louisa stood in the open doorway and watched them leave. She was concerned about her daughter, concerned about the rift with Henry and how it might affect their marriage. Minnie's alacrity in suggesting a walk in the woods with the handsome timber buyer also troubled Mother Tornow. "Oh fiddle," she exclaimed to nobody but herself, slammed the door and stoically fired up the stove with another stick of dry hemlock, "I worry too much."

From the corner, young Mary asked as she played on the bed with her sister, "Where'd Ma go?"

"Gone berry pickin', I guess," Louisa said as she stared with a crestfallen gaze at the pails of berries they'd picked earlier. "Gone berry pickin' and didn't even take a bucket to put 'em in."

Returning from town later that afternoon, Fritz Tornow came into the cabin with a puzzled look on his face, "Who belongs to that fancy rig tied to the rail?"

Louisa tried to remain casual as she continued to prepare supper. But anxiety cloaked every word, "Belongs to a timber buyer, name of John Kennedy, who came lookin' for you."

Fritz swept Mary and Lizzie up in his arms as they ran to him in their child-like joy, "Grandpa, grandpa."

"Where's Minnie?" Fritz asked.

"She and the timber buyer went down by the river."

"What are they doin' down there?"

"Pickin' blueberries."

Soon the elder parents heard the giggling voices of Minnie and John Kennedy returning. The Tornow boys had gotten home from school and were tending to their chores in the barn. Fritz walked out to meet the couple, a serious scowl spread across his bearded face.

"Hello, Pa," Minnie said, staring with embarrassment at the ground.

"Mr. Tornow, I stopped by to talk about you selling your logs direct to me," Kennedy said with an air of confidence as he buttoned his Donegal tweed jacket.

"Not interested," the patriarch spit out the words cuttingly.

"Well, thanks anyway," Kennedy replied, as he untied his horse and climbed into the buggy. He couldn't get away fast enough, he'd seen the hard look in Fritz' eyes, a threatening look that frightened him.

Fritz wanted to say so many things to his daughter that he decided not to say anything. He might lose his temper. They walked to the cabin where Louisa was waiting at the open door. She didn't even bother to ask Minnie if they had picked any berries. The answer was obvious.

"We had a nice walk but I'd better take the girls and git home. I'll use the shortcut trail," Minnie said, shooing the youngsters towards the door.

"You'd best comb your hair first," Fritz said. Long shadows and cooler air reminded her darkness was near. She hurried along the trail towards home through the timber. Minnie hated going back. Henry had such a temper she never knew what he might do. He was sure to discipline her for coming home late. But on this day it wouldn't matter. It had been worth anything he might do. Walking and talking with such a sophisticated man as John Kennedy would make up for any abuse Henry might dish out. At the top of a slight rise, a rustling in the huckleberry brush alarmed Minnie.

She stopped, nerves on edge, her eyes frantically searched for the cause of the frightening noise. As she held tight to Mary and Lizzie's little hands, her heart was racing out of control. Was it a guilty conscience that made her think Henry might be coming to punish her?

"What is it, Mama?" five-year-old Mary asked. Before she could answer, a sleek deer bounded out of the bushes and up the trail, twitching it's tall, attentive ears, frightened by Mary's voice. Minnie breathed a deep sigh of relief.

"Come on girls, let's us hurry home."

Back at the Tornow homestead, Fritz and Louisa were sitting outside the cabin on sawed tree rounds improvised for seats. It was an unusually warm October evening. The balsam fragrance of the nearby evergreen forest floated on the twilight breeze. Fritz lit his venerable pipe, puffing out clouds of blue smoke as he said,

"Minnie shouldn't have gone off with that Kennedy fellow."

"I can't even imagine why she done it," Louisa said.

"She warn't thinkin'," he replied.

* * *

In the darkness, the yellow lantern glow in the Bauer cabin window sent a sharp twinge through Minnie's attractive body like a jolt of electricity. Oh, Lord, she thought, he's a'waitin' for me.

Henry was sitting in his favorite rocking chair and the girls raced to him and climbed up into his lap. He paid little attention to them but raised his eyebrows towards Minnie.

"I s'ppose you been with your kinfolk again."

"Helpin' Ma can blueberries," she said. Taking off her sweater she hung it on a wooden peg behind the door.

"When was you plannin' to fix my supper?" he asked with an angry scowl.

"Won't take but a shake, the makin's are all set to heat."

"I'm gittin' sick and tired of you spendin' all your time over there. If this happens again there'll be hell to pay," the German elder hissed as his face turned a bright red, as red as the beets Minnie was warming on the stove.

Minnie busied herself preparing supper and thought, well that weren't half bad. Guess he's too worried 'bout his supper to git hard-boiled with me.

Thanksgiving came and went, Christmas saw the homesteaders almost buried beneath three feet of snow. Most of it was still on the ground when they turned the calendar over to 1892. The inclement weather kept John Tornow from tramping the woods with Cougar, but they spent a lot of time curled up in the barn's hayloft. Ma wouldn't allow his dog in the house but that was alright. The little cabin was crowded. He felt better away from the tightly massed family members, anyway.

When the winter rains relented the family was busy getting the crops into the ground. Everybody worked together, shoulder to shoulder, sowing the seeds that would put food on the table.

Despite Henry's ranting and raving, Minnie continued visiting her folks, often walking the shortcut trail. Early one afternoon in February she was enjoying a cup of tea with her mother and gossiping at the large, hand-hewn Tornow table. Louisa gawked in surprise as Minnie dropped a casual remark. "I've gotta get into town real soon and see the doctor, Ma. I'm pregnant again."

* * *

The Tornow family's farm income was derived from selling the limited overabundance of produce; potatoes, rutabagas, a few eggs, some hay when the crop was generous. These earned dollars purchased necessary staples at the General Store; lamp oil, flour, sugar, salt, soda, tea and coffee. The farm was now producing sufficient crops, over and above the family's needs, to earn extra money.

During early spring of 1892, Fritz Tornow increased his logging operation. He was fed up with just keeping his head above financial quicksand, living a hand-to-mouth existence. He owed the bank, the General Store, and a long-term debt back in Germany. He didn't like owing people. Not one bit. His greatest asset was the old-growth timber on the homestead and he began converting this crop into cash. That year with the help of his sons, Fritz cut enough timber to pay off the debts and stash away a few dollars in the Montesano State Bank. He also began buying lumber at the sawmill to start construction of a larger house to accommodate the family.

Minnie was afraid to ask her husband to take her into town for a visit to the doctor, afraid of risking his ire. She asked Fritz one day, "Pa, next time you're headed that way, can I ride along with you?"

"Sure, Honey," he replied, "matter of fact I'm goin' in tomorrow. Come on over in the morning."

It was early March, 1892, an unusually balmy day in the Pacific Northwest for that time of year. Fritz and Minnie braved the muddy country road for a trip into Montesano. The German father shopped the town's main street while his daughter visited the doctor's office. Minnie came out of the small, one-room building, head hanging low, walking lethargically to the buggy. Climbing in she said, "Just as I thought, I'm pregnant, due in July." Fritz was at a loss for what to say. He didn't know if this was good or bad news for his daughter. "Well, maybe it'll be a boy this time, Honey."

Minnie feared telling Henry about her pregnancy, but decided to spring the news that night at supper. "I rode into town today with Pa and went to the doctor. I'm pregnant, due in July sometime."

He was at first proud that he had fathered another youngster. Maybe this time she'll produce a son to help me with the work, he thought. But then the German farmer paused and reflected on past events. We ain't been sleepin' together all that much. At once a dreaded suspicion that he might not be the father crossed Henry's jealous mind. His jaw squared, flesh tightened, and his eyes narrowed in contemplation.

* * *

John Tornow was glad to see summer arrive. It meant no more school for a few months, he could get away from people, get off in the woods with Cougar, all alone. Soon he'd be a teenager. He began staying away from home for days at a time. The young adventurer roamed ever further into the precipitous Olympic Mountains, laying down to sleep with Cougar wherever nightfall overtook them.

As he wandered, John began to notice the still, small voice from within himself, a haunting, invisible companion that seemed to always be tagging along. *Don't you suppose your Ma and Pa worry about you when you're out here alone? They want you home. Then Edward could pull some of his tricks on you, could blame you for things you didn't do. And your Uncle Henry, he's another reason to stay away from home. The way he treats all the family, but especially Minnie whom you love so much, almost as much as you love Ma. Makes you really mad!* Poor John, suffering so from insecurity.

Sometimes it got so loud John had to slam his palms over his ears in an attempt to quiet the voice. That often didn't work very well. The words just about drove him crazy.

By early June, Minnie Bauer's pregnancy was very obvious. She ballooned with imminent motherhood. Minnie made arrangements with Louisa to come over and be her midwife for the birth.

Just after the Fourth of July, Minnie could tell it wasn't going to be much longer. On the morning of the sixth, Henry was out hoeing spuds so she told Mary, "You'll have to go git Grandma. Take the trail through the woods and tell her the baby's a'comin'."

Minnie's labor was brief. A bit after noon the baby's head emerged. With deftness learned from frontier experience, Louisa delivered the little boy then toweled and swaddled him. As the afternoon sun pierced the dim light within the little cabin, the stillness was pierced by the first shrill cries of the infant. With loving tenderness, Louisa tucked the baby into bed beside his mother.

"Ma, somethin's wrong down there."

Louisa bent to look. "Oh my God, Daughter, there's another one. You got twins." Scurrying for more towels, she cared for the second boy and with deep affection put him in bed on the other side of her daughter. The two infants peeked out from the woolen blankets, their tiny red faces squinting at their unfamiliar surroundings. Minnie spread both arms around her new babies, drawing them closer to her bosom, a pallid but satisfied smile on her face.

Henry accepted Louisa's presence, even thanked her for assist-

ing with the delivery. She spent the next few days at the Bauer cabin helping Minnie with her newborn twin boys.

It was almost a week before Minnie told her mother she had picked names for her sons.

"Me and Henry had a little set-to about what we was gonna name 'em," Minnie said. "But we settled it, he named one, I named the other."

"So what's their names?" Louisa asked.

"He picked William."

"What did you pick?"

"John."

This name took Ma Tornow's memory back to the handsome timber buyer. Then a logical thought came to mind. "Named him John after your brother, I'll wager," she said, beaming an expectant smile.

"Well, yes, I guess so."

One hot summer morning a couple of months after the twins were born, John Tornow took the shortcut trail, pausing at the edge of the Bauer's timber. With apprehension he parted the fir boughs just enough to get a clear view of their cabin without being seen. Patiently, he watched for almost an hour. It was Friday. Uncle Henry often went into town on Friday. John waited. A feisty bluejay in the top of a bushy, western white pine tree raucously scolded him, threatening to disclose his presence where he hid in the tall oat grass.

John began to worry. What would happen if Uncle Henry caught him out here? He urgently wanted to see his Sis and the twins, but not while the elder Bauer was home. He'd seen enough of his meanness, didn't want to see no more.

Soon the lad's patience was rewarded. Henry came out, harnessed the mare to the buggy and drove down the dusty dirt road to town.

Montesano's venerable courthouse displays the bronze plaque honoring the memory of slain deputies, Colin McKenzie and Al Elmer.

"I ain't seen you for so long, Baby Brother, how you been?" Minnie asked as John wiped his shoes and shuffled into the cabin.

"Fair to middlin', Sis, I came over to see the babies," he said, sniffing the delightful aroma of his sister's fresh baked cookies.

She led her brother to a wide wooden crib Henry had made, wide enough for both babies. John leaned over the crib to get a better look, a proud glint in his eyes. "They sure is cute, which one is John?"

"That one," she pointed, "do you want to hold him?"

"Gol, Sis, can I?"

"Sure, they won't break."

Tenderly as lifting feathers, she nestled the baby in John's arms. "There, that's your new nephew, your first after two nieces, say hello to him."

"Just look at this little feller and he has my name too."

John stayed at the cabin for most of the day, wolfing down half-a-dozen of Minnie's homemade cookies, leaving only when he feared Uncle Henry was due back. He left with reluctance, giving Minnie, Mary, Lizzie and the twins a big kiss goodbye.

* * *

In December a northern storm from Canada ravaged Western Washington, plummeting the temperature down near zero. Lakes and ponds froze while billowing plumes of smoke rose from most homesteader's chimneys as wood burning stoves and fireplaces roared blazing red to maintain cabin warmth. Ice-heaves decorated the ground like hardened cake frosting and walking sounded like crunching through a sack of walnut shells. The usual muddy road past the Tornow homestead froze solid, giving it the hardness of concrete.

On a cold, bright, cloudless day, Fritz told Louisa, "I've got some errands in town and with the road frozen, it might be a good time to go tend to 'em."

"You'd better bundle up, that sun looks a lot warmer than it is," she cautioned.

Fritz first stopped at the General Store for supplies. He handed the crumpled shopping list to an aproned clerk who began filling the order from the shelves that extended up to the ceiling.

"We got a real good price on Sperry Flour this week," the grocer pitched Fritz. "Can you use a hunnert for only three dollars?"

"I'll take one. Never could turn down a bargain."

"Got everythin' now 'cept the coal oil. I'll fill your can out back then tote up the bill and we can begin loadin'."

Later, the Tornow elder strolled down Montesano's plank sidewalk, peering into the shop windows.

Poking around Jackson's Hardware store, a used rifle on the gunrack caught Fritz' eye. It was a Winchester Model 73 lever-action carbine, .44/40 caliber. Just what John would want for Christmas, the father thought as he longingly eyed the rifle. He wondered how much it would cost, just one way to find out.

"Will you haggle on the price of that rifle?" Fritz asked the proprietor. "For you I will," he said. "Asking thirty dollars but for cash money you can have 'er for twenty-five."

"I was thinkin' more like twenty."

"Twenty? I paid more for it than twenty. How about twenty-three dollars and I'll throw in a box of cartridges and we can still be friends."

"I'll take your cartridges and we can be friends for twenty-two dollars."

"Well, alright. You drive a hard bargain, Fritz. Need any gun oil?"

"Got lots," he said, plunking down the money for his son's Christmas present. Then he remembered the others. He bought a gift for each including a jackknife for Edward and a new tailor-made rolling pin for Louisa to replace the handmade one she'd had for many years. It never was perfectly round. The black walnut tree trunk Fritz had carved it from had been somewhat warped out of shape.

For Christmas the entire family bundled up and tramped down by the river to cut an aromatic, noble fir from the forest. They squeezed it into one corner and decorated it with strings of dried, red berries. The fragrant balsam aroma floated into every niche and corner of the small cramped cabin, reminding them of the fresh, clean outdoors. Louisa made stollen and streusel, just like an old-country Christmas.

John was completely overwhelmed with the rifle and he gave both his parents a big kiss. "Ain't nothin' in the whole wide world I'd have liked better," he beamed.

Edward was happy with his jackknife but cast a jealous look at his brother's rifle, wishing Pa had given him one too.

The following day Fritz noticed John working in the barn so he went out to investigate. "What you doin' son?"

"I'm takin' the sights off my rifle, Pa, don't need 'em no more since you learned me to shoot by feel. Now I shoot quicker'n straighter."

* * *

By the late 1890's Fritz had finished building the new house. Almost four times larger than the original log cabin, the family now had
ample sleeping space for everyone. At the turn of the century, John
had grown up like his brothers. He was now twenty years old, a strap-
ping six footer, almost two hundred pounds. He was broad-shouldered
and muscular, somewhat like the bare-knuckle boxers of the era. From
time to time he worked as a logger for local timber companies, usually depositing his earnings in the bank. John's monetary needs were
small, a box of cartridges occasionally; seldom did he buy new clothes
or shoes. As a result his savings grew, but he cared little for money.

And always the lure of the outdoors pulled him like a magnet to
the timbered hills and sweet-smelling valleys of the majestic Olympics. He was often gone from the home place and his preference for
a solitary existence worried Fritz and Louisa. One day in late fall, after
the crops had all been harvested, the German father told his wife,
"Maybe I'll take John trappin' for a couple of weeks, get closer to
him. Can you handle things here?"

"Sure, me 'n the boys will do just fine, you go ahead."

With Edward and Albert at home to help Louisa, Fritz and John
loaded their packsacks with provisions and traps, donned rain slickers, grabbed rifles, and with a whistle to Cougar were off to the
mountains. "Come on, Cougar, we're goin' trappin' with Pa," John
said, kissing his mother goodbye. "It'll be good riddance around here
to git that dawg out from underfoot," Louisa said in a pretended
tone of disgust.

The trail they took wound beneath towering old-growth conifers,
interspersed with mossy deadfall logs and sword ferns, salal brush
and huckleberry, that grew abundantly in the wet rain forest where
precipitation often exceeded ten feet annually. The lush, verdant
growth gave off a pleasant aroma like a heather meadow in spring-

time, a refreshing, clean smell. This was John's nirvana, these awe-inspiring foothills and mountains, the single place where he felt comfortably secure.

"We'll go try a little lake I know," Fritz told his son when they rested beneath a stringy-barked, towering cedar for a quick noontime meal. "There's a dinky lean-to shack on a small island where we can camp while we set out our traps," he said, flipping Cougar the last bite of his roast venison.

As they arrived at the marshy little lake, John heard the croaking melody from the horde of frogs residing around the copper-green, pondweed pads in the shallow, brackish water. "Must be a million of 'em," John said, grinning.

"I've heard some folks call it Frog Lake," Fritz smiled as an explanation for the rippling, watery serenade. He never knew, nor even imagined that the lake would one day be named for his son.

John and Fritz enjoyed several chats far into the night around the cheerful campfire. "I just don't know how to tell you Pa, but out here is where I feel best, not around people, especially Edward and Uncle Henry. I get troubled some by a small voice talkin' to me. Sometimes it's almost enough to drive me loony. I can't shut it up."

"Ain't nothin' wrong with that, but learnin' to deal with all kinds of people and feelings is just part of growin' up," Fritz told him. "You'll look at it different as you get older, I s'pect."

Mother Tornow was tickled to see them come home. "Land sakes just look at the two of you. I swear you're just like a couple of mountain men. Smell like 'em, too. I'll heat some bath water. Oh, that danged dawg come home with you? Well, git him outside where he belongs."

While everyone was out at the barn, Louisa slipped Cougar a morsel of baked venison from the previous night's supper. Then she was quick to glance around making sure nobody had seen her.

* * *

The tiny Bauer cabin was also becoming cramped for the family and Henry began building a two-story house nearby. They moved in around the turn of the century.

By this time, the Bauer twins, John and William, were eight years old, short and stocky, like a matched pair of chunky frontier bookends. They idolized their Uncle John Tornow who spent considerable time teaching them to love and understand the outdoors like he did.

Henry Bauer was a farmer, and a good one. He knew or cared little about the outdoors but recognized, and with reluctance, accepted that John was passing along his woods-lore to the boys. He couldn't be bothered to spend much time with them. And down through the years as he looked at his twin sons perhaps a tiny question of fatherhood crossed his suspicious mind. He made a business of conjecture.

Several times Edward Tornow tried to take over his brother's tutelage role with the twins, tried to step in and nudge John aside. But the youngsters always rebuked him with, "Oh no, Edward, Uncle John's showin' us all that kind of outdoor stuff."

John took the twins to the river and showed them where the biggest trout lurked in quiet water behind large boulders. In the fall, the trio caught sacks full of migrating Chinook salmon on their way to upriver spawning grounds. On balmy days, when vine maple leaves turned to golden-yellow and flaming red hues and began to flutter to the ground in stillness, the trio would lay on their backs in the stumpy, grass fields and count geese in the great migrating vee's that passed overhead. The twins learned about nature from their Uncle John; he taught them well and they adored him.

Another of Minnie and Henry's youngsters was also growing up on the remote homestead. By 1905 Mary had matured to become an attractive young lady of nineteen with a pleasing resemblance to her mother. She was mighty popular at the community hall dances held in the area and attended by the young people of the valley, including the Tornows, except, of course, John. Mary was sometimes in the company of Edward Tornow, four years her senior, but it was accepted as just good family fun and not looked upon as serious by most. However, Henry Bauer viewed their togetherness with pessimism. He didn't like it, not one little bit. In fact, he hated seeing them together.

When her father voiced his concerns about Edward to Mary she laughed and shrugged it off with a flippant toss of her head that tantalizingly swished her long dark curls, so reminiscent of her mother. "Oh Pa, we're just havin' fun. After all, Edward's my uncle."

One summer morning in 1905 Henry Bauer told Minnie, "I've got business matters to tend to in Matlock. Guess I'll be gone most of the day."

After Henry left, Minnie thought it would be a good opportunity for the kids to spend some time with their grand-mother, Louisa. "Mary, why don't you kids walk the trail to Grandma's while Pa's away?" she said. They agreed.

Henry found it a pleasant day for the drive into Matlock on the narrow, gravel road. He walked the horse slowly to avoid raising dust. He was admiring a colorful field of purple fireweed and common foxglove that had sprung up on a logged-off hill when a buggy approached from the opposite direction.

As they slowed to pass Henry didn't recognize the other driver. It had been almost fourteen years and then under less than favorable circumstances. But John Kennedy recognized Henry as their buggies passed. Make no mistake about that.

The timber buyer, now timber baron, owned large sections of valuable forestland and had just returned from a short stay in Europe. Seeing Henry reminded him of Minnie and he did some lighthearted reminiscing. During the ensuing years he'd only seen her a couple of times at the General Store, once at the community hall with her charming daughter. I wonder, he mused.

Within a couple of hours the Bauer elder arrived at the bustling little community of Matlock. Wagons and buggies were darting helter-skelter on the busy, dirt street. Most were homesteaders like himself. Henry drove past the hotel, past the shoemaker's shop, even past the General Store. He turned east onto the road out of Matlock. Grainy clouds of brown dust from the powdery dry, narrow street were stirred by the horse and buggy, then lifted on a gentle breeze.

He pulled up in front of a plain clapboard little house, tied his horse and knocked on the door. A young woman in a neat, low cut gingham dress recognized him and flashed a welcome smile as she opened the door. "Henry, how good to see you again," she said. "Won't you come in and have a cup of coffee with me?"

John Kennedy resumed driving down the road and continued his pleasant reminiscing. It had been a long time, a very long time. Well, why not? He would enjoy seeing Minnie again. He turned his horse onto the road leading to the Bauer homestead. As Minnie answered his knock he asked, "Remember me?"

Minnie couldn't believe her eyes. There he stood, wearing his pleated forestry pants, fashion-tailored dress shirt and an adorable smile. He looked no different than when last she saw him. Perhaps a bit grayer around the temples.

"I haven't seen you for a long time, John," she said, beaming a radiant smile. "Won't you come in? I just put a fresh pot of coffee on the stove and I have your favorite bread and jam."

As the timber baron strode past her and into the front room of the new home, Minnie drew a breath of the delicious fragrance from his just-washed body. It emanated a subtle hint of sweet-scented cologne. What a difference between this gentleman and a sod buster who bathed once a week whether he needed it or not.

"What have you been up to?" she asked, taking down her two best china cups and saucers from the cupboard.

"I've been rather busy in my timber business," Kennedy replied. "In fact, I just returned from a month's visit to Europe. But let's talk about you. What's happening in your life?" he asked. "I see you have moved into a bigger house."

"Oh, nothing much happens around here," she said, deciding not to mention the birth of the twins. "Can I fix you a slice of bread to eat with your coffee?"

"That would be wonderful," he said.

The couple sat on homemade wooden chairs in the parlor and talked well into the afternoon. Minnie enjoyed Kennedy's conversation which was on a higher intellectual plane than she'd ever heard from any of her family members, for sure above Henry's level.

The timber baron thrilled the back-country woman, telling of his far-flung traveling experiences, the people and strange customs he'd encountered. Hearing all these wondrous tales was a compelling and unique occurrence for this naive lady of the raw frontier.

✻ ✻ ✻

Mary Bauer led the way through the forest path, followed by Lizzie and her twin brothers. Louisa saw them coming and met them at the door. So did John and Edward. Especially Edward.

"Land sakes, come in and sit a spell," Mother Tornow said, pushing Cougar off the door stoop with the side of her foot. "Danged dawg."

While the womenfolk were visiting, John took the twins out to the barn where he had a surprise for them hidden in the haymow. He gave them each a brand new fishing reel he'd bought from a mail order catalogue.

"Wow, those are beauts, Uncle John," They shouted with excitement.

When they returned to the cabin, Mary and Edward were gone. "Where'd they go?" John inquired.

"Didn't you see them outside? They went lookin' for you."

John went back outdoors and looked around. He saw no one. He looked behind the barn, by the root cellar, the woodshed and the chicken house. He didn't look down the path to the river. He thought to himself, they wouldn't go that far. Would they?

Driving home that afternoon Henry had a self-satisfied grin on his large-featured Teutonic face for the first time in many months. He was quite pleased with himself.

When he saw the fancy buckboard tied to his hitching rail, he thought, I didn't know we was expectin' company. Who could that be? His Chessy-cat grin began to fade.

Henry slid down from the buggy's spring seat, landing on his scuffed heels in the powdery dust. As he tied his own horse to the hitching rail he couldn't help but admire the visitor's sleek mare and handsome buggy. The rig made his own look like a bone-bag pulling a scrap wagon.

Minnie heard the buggy pull up in the front yard. In apprehension she rushed to the window and peered out as Henry strode onto the porch.

"Is that your husband?" Kennedy asked.

"Yes," Minnie replied, throwing open the home's glass-paned front door.

"Oh, good, I can ask him if he wants to sell any timber," the visitor said in a casual tone.

Henry ignored Minnie, brushed past her and spotted John Kennedy sitting at his table, in his house, and with his wife.

"What in hell you doin' here?" he bellowed as he clumped his heavy, leather farmer boots across the uneven floor coming on like a raging tornado. Henry's face turned a bright crimson and the veins in his neck strained, two engorged, pulsating arteries ready to burst. Both fists were doubled like two pounding pistons poised to strike. The scene was one of impending violence. Henry was a mad man, enraged, full of hate and wanting to attack.

Chapter Four

AS HENRY APPROACHED HIM, JOHN KENNEDY STOOD UP. OUT OF nervousness he fingered the spotless, broad brim of his western Stetson as he turned his attention to the belligerent homesteader.

"I stopped by to find out if you might sell me some of your timber," Kennedy said in an offhand tone.

Stomping up to the timber baron with fire in his eyes, Henry thrust his face almost nose-to-nose with Kennedy. "I've told you before I'm not interested in selling my damned timber to you."

Even in this threatening moment, Kennedy turned to crazy thoughts. Phew, what terrible breath he has, it's strong enough to tie my horse to. I'll wager Minnie seldom kisses him.

"Yes, I remember, but that was a long time ago. I thought you might have changed your mind by now."

"Well I haven't and never will. Now, if you know what's good for you, you'll get outta this house. If I ever catch you around here again, I'll take my rifle to you. Better believe it."

"Very well," Kennedy said in a patronizing manner, "perhaps you will be in a more receptive frame of mind at some later date."

The jealous German husband eased over towards his Winchester hanging on the wall. He barked a one-word command, *"Out!"*

"Thank you for the coffee and bread, Minnie," the timber baron said, moving with alacrity towards the door.

All of a sudden Henry's anger got the best of him. As Kennedy turned to leave, the homesteader grabbed the pretentious visitor by his crisp, clean shirt collar. With one hand he lifted him off the floor, and shoved him with full force through the open door.

Minnie was cowering against the near wall and was fearful of her husband's menacing actions toward Kennedy. "Don't hurt him, Henry. He ain't done nothin'," she pleaded.

Hurrying across the porch to his buggy, the timber baron flinched at the loud crack of the door being slammed behind him. He could hear Henry's agitated voice turned toward Minnie.

Shaken by Henry's explosive ouster, John Kennedy recalled all the reasons he disliked the ill-tempered farmer. He untied his horse, looking with disdain at the Bauer nag and dilapidated buggy, its improvised canvas top, broken-spoke wheels, patched and dirt-encrusted harness. Kennedy kicked the dust from his polished boots on his buggy's step-up rather than dirty the immaculate, deep-pile carpet covering the floorboards. He gave a muted cluck to his sinewy, sleek brown mare that had won a blue ribbon at last year's state fair. Reining into a tight half-circle, he drove away from the Bauer home.

Kennedy's anger increased as he reviewed the venomous treatment suffered at the hands of a dirt-poor, uncouth farmer. Having attained a lofty, well-respected position in life, Kennedy was unaccustomed to such outrageous attacks. But, he'd remember. He wouldn't forget this day. Paybacks can be hell, and with his wealth, he could afford paybacks.

Henry had emerged from the cabin to speed the timber baron's departure. He now stood watching the little swirls of dust kicked up by Kennedy's buggy. With upraised fist he beat the air like he was pounding nails with an imaginary hammer. *If I ever catch you around my place again, I'll kill you,* he shouted at the vanishing buggy.

Stomping back into the house he slammed the door while casting a menacing look at Minnie. She had slumped into a chair, head in her hands, sobbing like her heart would break.

There was a noise at the door. Thinking it was Kennedy returning, Henry charged towards it with clenched fists. His four children stood at the doorway.

"Where you been?" he screamed.

"Who was that fellow driving away like his tail was on fire?" Mary asked, surveying the parlor's furniture in disarray.

He'd about had it with people who didn't respond to his questions. "Answer me," he yelled.

"We was just visitin' Grandma," one of the twins said.

"Over at the damned Tornows again, huh? Why does everythin' 'round here go to hell in a hand basket the minute I leave?"

"What's wrong with goin' to Grandma's?" William asked, in wide-eyed inquisitiveness. Henry strode over to Minnie, paused, raising his right hand over his head in a threatening gesture. He commanded, "Don't you ever let that joker in this house again, ya hear me?"

She drew back, putting her hands over her face for protection from the threatened blow. "I hear what you're sayin', but we was just havin' coffee and jawin'. Weren't doin' nothin' to get so riled up

The quiet crossroads community of Matlock today consists of a combination general store, gas station and post office.

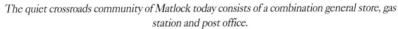

about." "Just remember what I'm tellin' you about that dandy," Henry replied.

The Bauer youngsters witnessed this parental conflict in quiet dismay. It hadn't been the first time they'd observed their father's temper tantrums. Probably not their last. But beyond a doubt the rampage, and other similar abhorrent actions, would stamp a negative imprint on their fragile young memories.

* * *

During the next few years John Tornow spent more time living in the forested foothills of the rugged Olympic mountains. Just him and Cougar. They roamed the wilds like homeless nomads.

He was a man now, twenty-seven years old. John's adolescent years had vanished before he even realized his youthfulness was gone. Gone before he'd enjoyed being a kid. When John found a place to his liking, he built a shelter out of materials at hand. Sometimes he cut down small trees. A few shelters were made from weathered boards salvaged from abandoned trapper's cabins. Caves provided good shelter; one hideaway was even found in the hollow of a huge cedar tree. All of John's dens were hidden in out-of-the-way places, well-concealed. A visitor would seldom just stumble onto one of his hangouts; they were camouflaged to blend in with the surrounding forest.

He accumulated bits and pieces of survival essentials; an old blanket, an empty lard can, a chipped cup or a battered wash pan. Things he found or scrounged as he meandered the timbered hills, creek bottoms and abandoned homesteads on the edge of civilization. Before long each shelter was stocked with bare-bones implements needed for extended visits.

He began staying away from home for a month at a time, then six or eight weeks. When his parents begged him to stay, he replied, "Me and Cougar like bein' alone out there. Ain't no reason to fuss or

worry none 'bout us."

The Tornow homestead was a quiet place now. Edward was the only son living there. He helped Fritz with the farm and once in awhile the other boys would come home from their outside jobs to help log some of the homestead timber.

The laborious years of homesteading were beginning to take their toll on the Tornow elders. They had raised a family under difficult circumstances, scratching out a bare existence from a less than cooperative environment.

An experienced timber cruiser stopped by for a cup of coffee with Fritz one day. "I run across John every once in awhile, or at least see where he's been," the fellow reported. "I think your son knows where almost every section corner in the county is located. He's got a keen eye for quality timber and knows who owns what out there."

On one of his infrequent visits back home, John told his father, "I've got my eye on a chunk of timber I'm hankerin' to buy. Would you go into town and help me get it?" John had saved his meager wages and trapping income, building up a sizable bank account. He had no trouble paying cash for the forested quarter-section of land, shelling out hundreds of dollars for timber later worth thousands.

On this same trip into town, John picked out a new rifle at the hardware store. His old .44/40 was nearly worn out. "The riflin' grooves in the barrel are plumb gone," he told Fritz. Then with a grin, he added, "When the bullet flops 'round in that smooth bore, I suspect it just tumbles out end over end. John selected a U.S. .30 calibre lever-action rifle, a popular model at the time. Arriving home from town, John went to the workshop and removed the rifle's sights.

"You're still shootin' by feel, I see," Fritz said, watching his son remove the iron sights.

"You taught me good, Pa," he winked at his father.

After a brief visit with his mother and Minnie, John packed up a few provisions and prepared to leave. "Goodness gracious, Son, why don't you stay home for awhile?" gray-haired Louisa asked, in her best motherly tone.

"I'm better off out in the woods," John replied. He loaded up his packsack, grabbed his new sightless rifle, several boxes of ammunition, and whistled for Cougar. The pair struck out the narrow, worn path past the barn and into the forest. It would be the last time he would see his father alive. Had he known, would he have stayed home? Probably not.

The toilsome life of a homesteader as he scrabbled with an unyielding land, and worked torturous hours with insufficient rest at last caught up with Fritz Tornow. He died on August 12, 1909 at the age of sixty-five.

Fritz was buried in a simple ceremony at the Grove Cemetery, a scant three miles from the homestead that had become the culmination of his quest for freedom in his chosen land. He attained final liberation, eternal peace in a quiet remote resting place carpeted with native orchard grass and bordered by tall Douglas firs. Fritz would have liked that. The old cemetery alongside the Brady-Matlock road today remains much as it was ninety years ago. It is still cared for by the few local residents.

All the family and most neighbors attended the patriarch's funeral. Almost everyone but John. Roaming the wilderness with Cougar, he had no communication with his family. The Bauer twins, out of love for their uncle, searched his usual haunts in the forest for several days trying to find John and inform him of his father's death, but they couldn't locate him. Weeks later he heard the sad news.

Nobody knows for certain when John learned that his father had willed him $1,700 from the estate. It might seem like an insignificant amount, but in today's dollars it would be the equivalent of almost $25,000. While John seemed to have little use for money, it was said there were others who coveted his assets.

Newspaper stories of the era told that John Tornow was institutionalized in a mental sanatarium in Oregon around 1909. The historians never found proof of this, or anyone who might have been responsible for trying to put him away. The only possible shred of believability to the sanitarium episode could have been provided by the assumption that by declaring John insane, those who sought his estate would thus be provided access.

Following the death of Fritz Tornow, only two members of the family resided at the farm—Louisa and her youngest son, Edward, John's wily, twenty-seven-year-old brother. A month or so after his father's passing, Edward developed a plan. At the next community hall dance, he seized upon the opportunity to put his plan into action.

As usual, vivacious Mary Bauer, now a grown-up girl of twenty-three was the center of attraction among the young swains of the upper Satsop Valley. Edward was one of Mary's favorites so he had no trouble getting a dance with her. As they glided across the floor Edward said, "Since Pa died I sure could do with someone to look after Ma. I could work it out to pay you a little somethin' each month and I'd enjoy your company, too. What do you say?"

"I'd care for Grandma. Then you'd have more time for farmin'. I'm most grateful you've asked. When do you reckon I should start?"

"How about right tonight when I take you home? You could pack a few things and come over to the house with me," Edward replied with a satisfied grin.

News of this arrangement hit the Henry Bauer household with the impact of blowin' a stump with a charge of black powder. The snarling, elder Bauer pulled down his .45/70 from the wallrack and stomped towards the door.

"Hold on," Minnie cautioned him, "ease up a mite. You ain't

gonna just traipse over there with your gun. Let me go talk with Mary. Maybe I can talk her into comin' home."

"Min, you know he's been hankerin' after her all along. She's such a nit-wit for goin' over there and lettin' him take advantage of her. I can't believe she's my own daughter. Blazes, she must be daft."

Minnie didn't get any satisfaction from Mary who told her mother in no uncertain terms, "I ain't comin' back Ma. There's too much devilment goin' on over home. I'm at peace here with Edward and Grandma."

"O.K., have it your way. I'll send John and William over with your belongin's. You're on your own. Guess that's that."

And so the Bauers lost their daughter. Lost her forever.

After Minnie told Henry about Mary's contemptuous refusal to return home, he picked up his rifle and headed out the door.

"You ain't fixin' to go over there, are you?" Minnie asked. "No," the elder Bauer replied in sorrow, "I give up."

Within a few minutes Minnie heard shots from the hillside as she kneaded the dough for a batch of bread. She knew what her husband was doing but glanced out the window anyway. Up in the stump patch, as if possessed, Henry was firing with reckless abandon at a dead stump.

She knew of his frustrations, of his deep distrust of the Tornows, and now Edward had their daughter, their little girl. Henry shot non-stop, over and over at the same stump. He was pretending. The stump represented all his inhibitions, and everyone who spurned him.

* * *

"You got him, nice shot," John Tornow said as he walked towards his hunting partner. "I wasn't sure if'n you'd saw him so that's why I whistled to get your attention. He's a nice four-point blacktail."

Ora Watson, a longtime Montesano furniture merchant, short

96

and stocky, was a good friend of the Tornow family. He especially enjoyed hunting with John. On this day John had guided Watson to a patch of green spruce trees where he knew several big bucks often bedded down.

"He always knows where to find deer," the furniture dealer later told his cronies as he puffed on his favorite stogie. "There's not a person in the county that can shoot better than John Tornow. I've seen him standing in the back of a moving wagon, bouncing over a rutted road and nail a running deer two hundred yards away," he told his fascinated audience. "He's absolutely uncanny with a rifle and the strange part about it he never aims, just shoots by instinct. On top of it all, I like the fellow," Watson continued. "He's a real gentleman and fun to be with. Sure, he avoids people, prefers to be alone, so what? I do too sometimes."

* * *

Nearly another year passed but few changes occurred around Matlock or the Tornow-Bauer homesteads. John Kennedy never forgot the roughing up he received at the hands of Henry Bauer when he pushed him out of the house. He often thought about revenge.

How can I get even with that sod-buster? Kennedy thought to himself. I've got plenty of money to pay someone to teach him a lesson. It would be expensive but maybe worth the cost.

Then he decided to buy a rifle and learn how to use it. He'd never owned a gun. A self-satisfied sneer crept over his handsome face as he pictured himself holding Henry Bauer at bay. He would point the gun at his midsection as the farmer begged for mercy and Minnie watched in admiration. He could do it. He knew he could.

* * *

John Tornow and Cougar had been away on one of their longer stays in the remote wilderness. Cold winds and rain clouds swooping down from the mountains gave hint that winter was not far away. John had shot a fat elk cow and had smoked a good quantity of the meat over a seasoned alder fire. He was preparing his larder for the lean times ahead.

They were sitting around a campfire at one of his remote hideouts one night, just talking, man and his dog. Cougar approached his master on faltering steps, gave a deep sigh, and flopped down beside him. "Yeah, I know, your rheumatiz is botherin' you again. Ain't neither of us gittin' any younger. You're almost nineteen now, I ain't too far from thirty."

John rubbed behind the old dog's droopy ears. The hound loved it when his master stroked him like that. With a show of gratitude, eyes half-closed, reflecting his blissful ecstasy, he projected a look of trust and devotion towards John.

"I wish I could git along with people same as you and I git along," the forest loner told his dog. "Seems like you understand everythin' goin' on with me. When I hear that ugly voice talkin' in my head, I think you hear it too. Sure do wish we could shut it off."

The aging floppy-eared dog stared with understanding at his master through his soleful hound's eyes. He understood every word.

"We've got a lotta meat now, maybe we should go home and visit for a couple of days before old man winter blows in. We could use another blanket or two out here, maybe even get one for you. Could take Ma and Min some of our smoked meat."

At the Tornow home Mary Bauer was skinning potatoes for supper when she looked out the window and saw John and Cougar approaching. "Good heavens," she exclaimed to Louisa who was now often bed-ridden. "Here comes Uncle John with his dog." Wiping her hands on her apron, Mary went to the door.

A faint smile slowly formed on Louisa's sallow face as she thought how nice it was going to be to see her son again. "Ain't seen John for quite a spell," she said. "Make sure the dawg stays out."

John had a good visit with his mother, Mary, and even Edward was civil towards him that evening when he came up from harvesting corn from the field by the river. John stayed for supper, even spent the night and enjoyed a big breakfast the next morning at Mary's invitation. But he soon had his fill of civilization and his brother's comments.

Preparing to leave, John told them about Cougar's worsening infirmity and lameness caused by the rheumatism. "He ain't doin' well, I'd like to leave him here if I could."

Edward was silent. Mary told John, "Sure, I'll feed him when I feed our dog, Rex. They get along O.K. sleepin' in the barn."

From the corner bed came, "Just so long as the dawg stays outside."

"Yes Mama."

John was nostalgic about leaving the homestead, the place where he had grown up, the place he remembered for so many experiences, both good and bad. He felt sorrow at leaving his mother, in light of her frail condition. But worst of all, he regretted having to leave his faithful friend behind; Cougar, his constant companion of nearly nineteen years, his dog who had been at his side all that time with unwavering loyalty.

Preparing to leave he kissed his mother on her dry, wrinkled cheek and squeezed her weak, bony hand. "Bye, Mama."

"Take care of yourself, Son." She had a strange apprehension it might be the last time she would see her nomadic boy. The thought brought a tear to her clouded eyes that she quickly brushed away. Oh dear, have I been a good mother? Louisa thought to herself. The measles, the fever, the friction among the brothers. Did I do all I could for my special son? And Louisa wondered, was it her fault that he turned his back on civilization? Was she responsible for his severe childhood illness and did it make him the loner she saw leaving

A road in the upper Satsop River valley has been named after the Tornow family.

today? She hoped not. She had many questions but few answers.

Outside, John bent down on one knee and threw his arms around Cougar's muscled neck. As he gave him a firm hug, the dog whimpered a small, forlorn cry, almost as if he knew what was coming.

"No, not this trip ol' man, you gotta stay here. We'll both hate it but it'll be better this way. I'll miss you, surely I will," he said as his emotions began to spill over.

John shed his first tear in many years, tears of sorrow in leaving the farm, tears for his mother and for his beloved companion. He straightened up to his full six feet, shrugged his shoulders into his packsack, grabbed his Winchester and with a heavy heart but not a backward glance, struck out on the familiar path behind the barn. As he disappeared, Cougar howled a mournful wail, expressing the pain he experienced seeing his master leave without him.

John detoured by the Bauer farm-home to see Minnie and the kids before returning to the wilderness.

"Henry's gone to town so come in and have a cup of tea with us," Minnie said. The twins, now eighteen, roughhoused with their Uncle and the two of them managed to wrassle him to the floor.

"I give up," John said laughing, "you guys are gettin' too goldarned big for me to handle anymore."

"Why do you have to go back out to the woods?" Minnie asked in a pleading voice. "Can't you stay to home with them what loves you?" John just smiled. He understood, so did Sis.

By the time he left the Bauer cabin, it was getting late so he decided to spend the night at the hideout; the cave where he and Edward had once enjoyed many frolicking boyhood adventures. He built a fire in the same rock-encircled fire ring where they'd roasted the chickens. Those chickens. Were they the main reason for the rift that developed with Edward?

As he sat at the cave in front of the fire that evening the bothersome little voice suddenly talked to him. *Did you try to be friends with Edward or are you as much to blame for the heartaches you're both feeling?* "I did all I could, it surely wasn't any of my doin's," John said aloud. As he looked around he felt foolish. He'd forgotten Cougar wasn't there to talk to. Then the impact of his dog's absence fell hard on John. He hung his head in his hands and cried a few tears of despair. He realized from now on he'd be alone.

* * *

John was stretched out on a dry bed of fluffy forest moss one day in November of 1910. He laid comfortably listening to the pounding rain bouncing off the weather-tight lean-to he'd constructed in a hidden valley of the Olympic foothills. It was so remote nobody other than John had ever visited this tucked away sanctuary. It was in a small dead end canyon that branched off the main trail near the river.

Peering outside through the cracks between the logs of his crudely built shack, he saw a saturated landscape that was drenched from the continuous downpour. This was Pacific Northwest rain, droopy, soggy, dense moisture, straight off the ocean.

In an instant, through the noise of the downpour, John heard a shot, sounded like a rifle shot. He cocked his head sideways, listening. There was another shot. What did it mean? He jumped to his feet, pulled on a tattered knee-length raincoat he'd found beside the railroad tracks, donned a sou'wester hat, grabbed his Winchester and stepped out into the rainstorm.

Within a half-hour he had slogged through the deluge to the main trail from where the shots had been fired. Looking down from a rocky precipice he saw two men several hundred yards away coming up the trail. Then he recognized them; they were his nephews William and John.

He bounded in deer-like leaps down the steep bank to the path. The twins looked like a couple of drowned pups. "What in tarnation are you doin' out in this kind of weather?" he asked, hunched over with his back to the storm.

"We come lookin' for you, Uncle John." William said, emptying the water that had collected in the folds of his coat and hat, running down his rounded nose.

"Yeah, afraid we got bad news," nephew John said, a crest-fallen look on his water-streaked face. "Grandma died two days ago and Ma wanted us to come fetch you for the funeral."

John was devastated by the news. He hung his head and clenched his eyes shut, hoping this was a bad dream and he'd wake up to find it hadn't happened. Then reality set in.

"You boys turn around and head home before you catch your death of cold in this storm. I'll pack up and be on my way within the hour. Many thanks for comin' after me."

He turned and climbed back up the hill while the Bauer twins double-timed down the trail to get home before dark.

They had about ten miles to go but at their dog trot pace it wouldn't take them more than a couple of hours. They were young, strong, healthy kids.

Hiking back to his lean-to, John's had a queasy feeling in his stomach. Where would it all end, he thought to himself? Ma's dead. So soon after Pa? It was difficult to accept the tragedies that had befallen those he loved the most.

Nearing the top of the hill he clapped his hands to his ears. There it was again. The troublesome, small voice said, *These wretched happenings might be your fault, John Tornow.*

* * *

Once again the little group of pioneers gathered in the hushed stillness beneath the lofty fir trees at the Grove Cemetery. The rain had stopped but dark, threatening clouds were still high overhead. The day was as gloomy as the mood of the small assemblage. Several buggies, a spring wagon and a half-dozen saddle horses were tied at the hitching rail. The animals stood quiet as if they knew this was a solemn moment.

Louisa Tornow had died a couple of months short of her seventy-third birthday. More than the average age for the grueling lifestyle of the early settlers.

John had stopped at the homestead, enjoyed a tearful reunion with Cougar and changed clothes for the funeral. He'd borrowed a tailored jacket from one of his older brothers, donned clean shirt and trousers from his meager belongings stored in the upstairs bedroom.

Heads bowed, the Tornow brothers, John, William, Frederick and Albert stood in mourning. Edward and Mary were alone at the edge of the grieving crowd. The Bauer family was nearby and Minnie stepped over to embrace her brothers. There was a noticeable absence of mingling by Henry Bauer with any of the Tornow relatives.

Following the burial, Mary called Minnie and John off to the side. "Would you mind stoppin' by the house? I got somethin' to jabber about with you. Just you two, no others. Keep it under your hat."

A little later at the Tornow homestead, while Edward was out in the barn, Mary put on the tea kettle and set out a plate of German torten cookies. She said, "This is plumb hard to talk about. I'm so shameful. It appears that I'm pregnant and ain't got no husband. Guess I messed up but that's the long and short of it."

Minnie hung her head and sobbed, "Oh Mary, I'm so sorry."

John covered his face with his large weathered hands. Just one more misery for the family, he thought to himself.

"I wanted both of you to know." Mary said. "But please don't tell Pa. No tellin' what he might do when he gets his dander up. Edward knows and I've told my brothers but that's all. The twins know who the father is but I ain't tellin' no one else and that's that. We've already had more devilment in this family than you can shake a stick at."

"What are you gonna do, Mary?" her mother inquired, weeping into her embroidered handkerchief.

"Uncle Edward said he'd take me into Aberdeen. Don't want to see no doctor around here. It would soon be all over the valley and I ain't proud of it. Guess I'm just betwixt and between," she replied, her large round, tear-filled eyes staring expressionless at the home's darkened wood floor.

With heavy hearts, Minnie and John left the homestead promising Mary they would keep her secret. After Louisa Tornow's passing, Edward was the last remaining member of the clan on the farm. Just Edward and Mary, Cougar and Rex.

John Tornow returned to his forest home that same day after again saying goodbye to Cougar. He was in a state of deep depression at the latest shocking news on top of the sorrow he was feeling for his mother's death. He gave considerable thought to Mary and her scandalous predicament. Shouldn't the father of the unborn child marry her? And who was it? He dared not even think of the possibilities. But, yet.

About a week later Mary went to Aberdeen and moved into a boarding house, a popular mode of habitation during the times. Her sister Lizzie had taken a job and was living in the booming lumber town where sawmill smokestacks obscured the environs, belching forth the heavy, black smoke of timber processing. The pregnant girl became violently ill towards the end of November and consulted a well-known physician. It was reported the doctor performed an abortion on the homespun country girl from the Upper Satsop Valley. She died from a botched, illegal operation on December 1, 1910. It was yet another sorrowful ordeal for the Tornow/Bauer families. How much more could they withstand? There'd be more. A lot more.

Once again the Bauer twins spent several days searching the wilds for their Uncle John, this time to tell him of their sister's death. But the country was too immense, too rough and isolated for them to locate the forest loner.

Mary had been a budding young girl, a beginning flower of womanhood, just twenty-four years old. Too young to die needlessly.

The epitaph on Mary Bauer's headstone, still visible today, appropriately reads: "The path of sorrow and that alone leads to the land where sorrow is unknown."

Henry Bauer was deeply despondent over his daughter's death. As he and Minnie commiserated at home following the funeral, Henry said, "I should take my rifle to that son of a buck. All this misery is his doin'. If Mary'd stayed home, none of this would have happened."

"Cool down Henry," Minnie pleaded. "Don't jump at conclusions," she argued, grabbing her husband by the arm of his blue farmer's shirt. "If you go over there and do somethin' foolish, you'll spend the rest of your life in jail. It ain't worth it."

Minnie soon calmed her husband but she felt uneasy that he might sneak out and go seek revenge. She was worried. Once again his temper was controlling his actions.

After he cooled off, Henry conceded and put the rifle back on the rack, telling his wife, "You're maybe right, but the day's comin' I'm gonna get even with that Tornow brother." The next morning Henry was working in the barn after having a prolonged stump-shooting spree to ease his frustrations. Soon the twins, William and John, now eighteen years old, came down to breakfast.

Minnie was curious about what their sister had told them before her death. "Did Mary tell you boys how she got pregnant?"

They exchanged furtive glances, then, head hanging, William said, "Yes, Ma, she did."

"Did she tell you who the father was?"

At this question both boys just stared quietly at Minnie.

"Well, did she?"

"Yes Ma, she did," John said as if each word was like a blade cutting his tongue as he uttered it.

"Stop beatin' 'round the bush. Who was it?"

Now William assumed the role of spokesman, his lower lip began trembling as he declared, "Please Ma, in all due respect, Sis made us swear on our honor we wouldn't tell nobody. You gotta understand."

"I understand," Minnie said with a solemn look. "Does anybody else know who the father was?"

"Only the father," William said. "He knows."

The coroner ordered an autopsy on Mary Bauer to confirm the cause of death. The physician was arrested and charged with manslaughter. The trial was lengthy and created quite a stir in Aberdeen, Montesano, the county seat of Chehalis County, and especially in the Satsop Valley. Abortion details and trial proceedings were prime media hot buttons during an age when published sensational events were few and far between. The court room was packed to capacity with curiosity seekers.

Henry Bauer was a willing witness during the trial and all the sordid details were hung out to dry in front of an eager audience. Everything was disclosed except the name of the girl's miscreant. The doctor was convicted of performing an abortion and sentenced to just nine months to be served in the county jail. Upon appeal, Washington State Governor Marion B. Hay pardoned the physician after he had served only seven months.

* * *

With his string of well-concealed sanctuaries hidden back in out-of-the-way locations, John Tornow led a solitary existence during mid-December of 1910. One cold and clear day the sun beamed weak shafts of light upon a thin snowfall that had blanketed the Olympic foothills the night before. John suddenly remembered the small lake where he had trapped with his father many years ago. Even with the cold weather nipping at his nose, he decided to hike up to Frog Lake through a light dusting of powdery snow and do some trapping.

First, he detoured to a cache beneath a huge blow-down spruce where he had hidden his traps during the off-season. The gunnysack of Victor number one-and-a-half, double springs, was just as he'd left it almost a year ago. John transferred the snares to his packsack, relishing the cold, slippery steel on his bare fingers.

Just as before, when he was still fifty yards from the lake he could hear the loud chorus of croaking. When he broke through the timber to the water's edge, all of a sudden the frogs became silent at his intrusion. John chuckled. Not watch dogs, instead they were watch frogs, he thought, noticing a tall blue heron standing motionless as a statue near a clump of common mare's tail plants, hoping to find a minnow for lunch.

Late one day as he was preparing a slab of smoked salmon over a campfire at his shack on the lake's small island, a strange noise caught his attention. It wasn't really a noise, but instead a silence—the frogs had stopped croaking. An ominous silence. Then he spotted a solitary figure that had appeared at the water's edge across the lake.

John quietly picked up his rifle and with caution born of necessity, stepped out of the firs and hemlocks to get a better look at his visitor. Squinting his eyes in the late afternoon's low winter light, he didn't recognize the figure standing on the opposite shore. Who could that be? He wondered.

The man was dressed in outdoor work clothes, mackinaw jacket, wool stocking cap, caulked (hobnail) leather boots. He had a loaded packsack on his back. The stranger approached John, stuck out a stubby paw and introduced himself. "Good afternoon, I'm J.B. Lucas from Hoquiam."

"My name's John. John Tornow. Glad to meet you."

"Are you trapping, John?"

"Yessir, me and my Pa we discovered this lake a long time ago."

"Yes, it is quite remote."

"I was just fixin' some fish for supper, you're welcome to join me."

"Thanks, John, sounds good," the visitor replied. "I smelled those fish cooking clear down at the far end of the lake." He crowded next to the small campfire, soaking up the welcome warmth while he enjoyed the bracing smoke aroma of seasoned alder and western red cedar that John was burning.

Lucas spent the night at the little lean-to. He told John he was a land developer and was looking over the stands of timber in the Oxbow country of the Wynooche River. Next morning he was on his way. John never saw him again, but Lucas was destined to play a major role in John Tornow's life.

* * *

Spring of 1911 was a glorious time of year in the hills and forests of the Pacific Northwest. The harsh winter had been nudged into obscurity as the trees budded. Greenery sprang like magic from the forest floor and abundant sunshine threw a mantle of warmth over the countryside. Everything smelled fresh and clean on a cool breeze wafting down from the mountains.

Summer soon arrived and John began thinking about a return trip to the homestead. He wanted to see Minnie and the twins, find out how Mary Bauer was doing. It was August, she's probably had the baby by now, he thought. But most of all he longed to see Cougar, his beloved and loyal friend.

The Bauer twins had been hoeing potatoes in a field bordered by a surrounding grove of tall Douglas fir trees. Suddenly William raised up, "Look there, it's Uncle John," he said, wiping the sweat from his brow with a stained, brown handkerchief.

They raced across the field to meet him and had a good tussle right there in Henry's planted spud patch. Good thing he wasn't around. "Go on with you before I box your ears," John jokingly threatened as the twins circled him like hounds worrying a bear. William took playful jabs at his midsection when his brother distracted his uncle's attention.

Minnie gave him a rousing welcome, "It's so good to see you Baby Brother," she cried, shedding tears of happiness.

John was aghast when Minnie told him of Mary's untimely death at the hands of the abortion doctor. "I can't believe it, Min," he exclaimed. "When will the wretchedness end? What've we done to deserve all this misery? Is the good Lord punishin' us?"

"I think I'm bein' punished for all my past sins," Minnie said without explanation. "Mary's at peace now but Henry still loses his temper when he thinks back on your brother enticing her over there. I swear he's been fixin' to go over and square things up more often than not."

"It don't seem like nobody's got much good to think about Edward," John said, picking up his packsack and preparing to leave. "I'm gonna head over that way so I can see Cougar." As he approached the home-place John saw Rex, his brother's purebred hound, lazily dozing in the sunshine on the front stoop. He thought it was strange Cougar wasn't there. Must be in the barn, maybe sleeping in the manger, his favorite place. Lazy old hound.

John dropped his packsack and leaned his rifle against the home's outside wall. He wondered where Edward was. And Cougar. He went to the barn and called his dog. No answer. Odd. He walked back towards the house. Edward came out, "Hello mountain man."

"Hello," John said. "Where's Cougar?"

"Oh, your dog? Well I went huntin' down the valley last week and he was so slow he was holdin' everythin' up so I shot him. He's gettin' too old anyway."

John Tornow's jaw dropped as he took a step back. His eyes blazed with fire as he stared straight at his brother. Something deep inside of him suddenly snapped. *You shot my dog?* he asked with an incredulous look, biting off each word like hot chestnuts and spitting them out, one by one.

"Yes, he was gettin' too old," Edward repeated as he noticed with apprehension that John was moving closer to his rifle which was leaning against the house.

Again Edward heard the question repeated as if his brother didn't believe what he'd heard, "You shot my dog?" Somewhat louder this time. Those angry, cutting words seemed to slam into the wooden walls and reverberate even louder in Edward's ears.

Spitting malice with each cutting word, John said, "I suppose you'd have shot Pa when he was gettin' slow, if he hadn't died first. And Ma, I guess she died before you could shoot her. Ya don't shoot somethin' just because it's old and slow. You got no thought for nuthin' but yourself and your fancies. You're pure scum. I disown you. You're not my brother. You couldn't be. Never."

John picked up his Winchester from against the house, spun around and glared at his brother with an explosive look as he jacked a live cartridge into the firing chamber. "I can't believe you shot Cougar." As the words tumbled out, John realized his best friend was gone. Killed by his brother. Killed dead.

"Well, I've a notion to shoot you like you shot my dog. You ain't fit to live after all the evil things you've did."

Edward stared in horror as John slowly raised the rifle in his direction. Terrified, he saw the hatred, the fire in his brother's narrowed eyes. "Now you be careful, John, put that rifle down, let's talk about this," he said in a fearful tone.

"Ain't nothin' to talk about." John hesitated. He pointed the rifle at Edward's midsection. Gut high. With a slow, deliberate movement John turned. Rex was still dozing on the stoop. The crack of the rifle sounded like a full box of dynamite exploding in Edward's ear. He flinched, jumped a foot off the ground, then realized what John had done. Rex never felt a thing. He was dead with a bullet through his heart.

John jacked the empty cartridge out of the rifle's firing chamber. It fell smoking to the ground. He levered another live round into the breech. "Shoot my dog, will you? Now we're even."

On that August day in 1911, for the first time John Tornow's hatred had erupted in explosive action. He had curbed his anger enough not to take a human life. But it had been close. Very close.

He turned his back on the homestead, on his birthplace, on the good and bad memories, never to return. As he departed for the last time, he told Edward, "I'm goin' back into the hills. This time for good. Nobody had better come after me, you hear?"

The next day Edward Tornow journeyed to Montesano and met with Sheriff Ed Payette. "I want to swear out a warrant for the arrest of my brother, John Tornow. He's insane, almost killed me he did. He shot my valuable hound. I want him arrested and put away," he said waving his arms for emphasis.

Payette calmly filled out a form and told Edward, "We'll investigate this and see what needs to be done."

One of the bystanders in the office casually sauntered towards the Tornow brother. "I couldn't help overhearing your conversation

111

with the sheriff." Extending his hand he continued, "I'm J.B. Lucas from Hoquiam. I'm a land developer and I ran into your brother up in the mountains awhile back. He seemed perfectly sane at that time."

"Much obliged to meet you, Mr. Lucas," Edward said. "Somethin's happened to my brother of late. He ain't the same person. Don't know what's gotten into him," he said, letting the words drift away quietly like dry leaves in a summer breeze.

"That's too bad, seemed like a nice fella."

"If you're ever up the valley, stop and see me sometime. I might have a proposition for you," Edward suggested, a faint smile curling the corners of his mouth.

"I surely will," Lucas said, shaking hands with Edward. Following a brief half-hearted search for John Tornow, the sheriff made a statement that appeared in local newspapers:

"I have found the allegations concerning John Tornow to be practically without merit. He was reported to be demented and living a precarious existence in the Upper Satsop Country."

"Tornow is having a disagreement with relatives and has adopted his solitary existence presumably to soothe his feelings. He has a sizable savings account at the Montesano State Bank and is not liable to suffer. He will not be further sought by the sheriff's department."

And so Edward Tornow's attempt to have his brother put away was thwarted by law officers. Edward's motive behind the insanity charge was never clarified. Nay-sayers of the era and later history researchers put forth opinions, none of which have ever been substantiated.

* * *

The morning of September 3, 1911, was not unlike most mornings around the Henry Bauer farm. Minnie fixed her husband's breakfast and he began work at first light, harvesting spuds from the field near the barn. The nineteen year old twins, William and John, had slept in. They had been helping their father in the fields but he had

The Mary M. Knight museum near Matlock displays extensive memorabilia of the Tornow era such as this wood cookstove and hand-operated washing machine.

let them off that day. After all, it was Sunday, a day of rest for most people, but not for Henry.

Tempted by the sweet aroma of pancakes sizzling on the wood stove, the twins clumped downstairs to a big breakfast Minnie had fixed for them. Afterwards they stretched out on a daybed in the front room. Soon, William, fidgety as usual, got up and peered out the window. It had been raining the past couple of days. A wet Indian summer. But on this fateful day the sun had reemerged. "Come on, John, let's go bear huntin'," William told his brother, giving him a swat across the backside to get him going. "I seen bear sign on the open hillside we logged a couple years ago down towards the river. They been eatin' berries over there."

From the timbered plateau overlooking the Bauer homestead, a solitary figure was crouched out of sight behind a big windfall spruce tree. For the past couple hours, he had been stealthily watching the Bauer home. Waiting. He was patient. I've got lots of time, he muttered to himself.

A pine squirrel, perched cockily in a golden vine maple nearby, eyed him with suspicion. The four-legged sentry watched the stalker with apprehension, munching his morning breakfast of mountain hemlock seeds from a brownish-purple cone.

Trigger-quick the intruder raised up. Somebody was coming out of the Bauer cabin. He raised his rifle but quickly lowered it as the twins disappeared from his view behind the house. He saw they were headed towards the river—carrying rifles. Interesting, he thought, this could be even better than he'd planned. A devious smile crossed his coppery-brown face as he reflected on the possibilities.

The timberline, formed by a prolific stand of old-growth Douglas firs and western hemlock, stopped at the edge of the plateau but continued on top for about a mile towards the river. As the boys meandered without direction across the open, stump-littered flat, the stalker crouched down low and hurried along paralleling their route and slightly above them. As he stepped out, the sudden movement startled the pine squirrel and with raucous chattering it scolded him in no uncertain terms.

Soon the twins stopped and examined something on the ground. The intruder was just out of earshot when John said, "See there, it's bear droppin's alright, and this blackie has been feedin' on them red devil's club berries over on that hillside."

"Looks fresh, he can't be far away," William offered.

The threatening visitor took up a position behind a large fir stump on the edge of the clearing. Unhurried he laid the rifle across the stump, pointed towards the twins. The sun had now broken out from the gray clouds and shimmered off the cold, blue steel of the rifle barrel, highlighting the sinister weapon.

Hiding beside the stump in a crouched position, the intruder slowly moved the gun until he had the bead squarely on the closest figure, a scant two hundred yards away. Ahhh, a perfect shot, he thought to himself as he adjusted his wide brimmed hat to shield away the sun's glare. The nearest Bauer twin was now just a mite farther than a city block away. He couldn't miss at this distance. His finger tightened around the curved, steel trigger. He was ready, no question about it.

At the last instant, just the blink of an eye away from immortality, both boys disappeared into a patch of autumn-hued, ten foot tall vine maples. Damn, he thought, watching the far side of the narrow grove. They'll have to come out of there. I can wait. Got lots of time.

Chapter Five

THE PREDATOR KNEW THIS COUNTRY WELL. BROAD SHAFTS OF sunlight accented jewel-like water droplets clinging to the varied shrubs and evergreen tree limbs like a scattering of loose diamonds. Everything sparkled beneath the bright early autumn sunshine.

The relentless aggressor was not interested in attractive scenery on this morning. His attention was riveted on a patch of multi-hued vine maples a half-mile away where he'd seen two men disappear who had not reemerged. What were they doing? His black-center golden eyes swept the woodsy landscape for movement. It was seldom anything eluded his eaglelike gaze, especially on a bright morning, especially when he was hungry.

The diligent sentinel swiveled his sharp-nosed head in nearly a complete circle to determine he hadn't overlooked anything in his terrain. As a slight breeze drifted over him the raptor clenched his taloned feet tighter around his spruce limb perch. He braced himself like a sailor on a rolling deck. He continued his concentrated scanning, watching for breakfast. This red-tail hawk would be the only witness to the drama unfolding in the woodland below his lofty vantage point. The only witness, but what a shame. A witness who could never testify and provide the true account of what actually happened on that fateful September day. The day of infamy that would long be remembered in Pacific Northwest history.

This remote corner of Washington State, these lower foothills of the Olympic Mountains, were sparsely inhabited. Just a few stout-hearted homesteaders every few miles whose stubbornness kept them trying to scratch out a living from land Mother Nature intended for growing timber. The saw-log trees were almost gone from the lower climes, harvested by long-john clad loggers around the turn of the century. Less accessible forests, a few miles away in the steeper hills, remained untouched. In the logged areas, stumps and dense ground-hugging brush covered the rolling hills and deep valleys surrounding an occasional cleared field that had been grubbed to pasture land by determined settlers. A quiet countryside, mostly undisturbed by civilization which retained the green, woodsy smell of all outdoors.

A rotted log lay lengthwise in the vine maple thicket, attracting the attention of the Bauer twins. Crumbling away to rusty-red pieces of decomposed wood, the fallen tree would soon complete the dust-to-dust cycle. At the log's center, the broken, decayed pieces had been scattered over the damp earth like particles thrown to the wind.

"See there," William pointed to the strewn bits of crumbled wood, "old Blackie's been here. Been pawin' around in that rotten log for grubs."

John knelt on one knee examining the wood bits as if to disprove his brother's theory. "Yeah, you're right. Here's a track where he stood in the mud. I can see some ants and a few grubs he missed. Don't see how they can eat them things."

With his rifle at the ready, William bent over to examine bear tracks in the wet dirt. "Here's his trail leavin' the brush patch. Come on John, let's follow him."

On the ridge above the Bauer twins, the patient intruder rested against the bleached-white stump in a crouched position, eyes glued to the edges of the thicket where he knew the boys would have to reappear. A gentle breath of wind cooled his face, bringing faint noises to him from the grove of little trees. Cocking his head, the solitary

117

figure listened. He could hear voices. He could hear the boys talking. He smiled a repulsive little smile. They're in there, he thought, I'll just wait. When they come out, I'll show them. I'll show all of them. Only a disturbed psyche numbed by hatred and revenge could perpetrate the travesty about to occur.

The hawk flinched out of instinct. At the sharp crack of the rifle, he steeled his survival-trained muscles for either fight or flight. It wasn't a new sound to him, he'd often heard it emanating from the man-place homestead down the valley. But it threatened him, unlike the wilderness noises he listened for: the cooing of a dove; the rustling in the brush of a mouse or rabbit; a squirrel's chattering. Those were good sounds, food sounds. But he heard none this morning.

"You hit him, you surely did," William shouted at his brother as they ran down the ridge to get a better look into the canyon where the bear had disappeared into the forest understory after the shot.

A fresh crimson splatter on the obscure trail like a shiny spill of wet, red paint brought both boys to a halt. "See there, I told you so, fresh blood, he's hit hard and headin' for the canyon," William said, panting after the short run.

"We can stand on top that little orchard grass flat and see where he went," John suggested, "C'mon, hurry up before he gets away."

From the ravine they could hear the brush crashing from the bruin's headlong flight. They could even smell the trail of fear and trauma hanging in the air, marking the animal's hasty retreat.

The lone figure atop the ridge, looking every bit like a backwoods Simon Legree, muttered obscenities to himself as he watched his plan unravel before his eyes. First he couldn't see them. Then, when they came out of the thicket, they were running too fast. They stopped abruptly and he drew down on them, steadying his Winchester across the log. He no sooner had them in his sights than they took off running once more. Couldn't risk a running shot. But wait. They've stopped again. They're looking into that canyon for the wounded bear.

The bruin's jet black coat glistened in the morning brightness, shiny as a new pair of patent leather shoes. He plowed through the small trees and dense shrubbery like a runaway oxen team, desperate in his struggle to escape his relentless pursuers. He disregarded the stinging wound in his side, it wasn't important now. The bear hesitated for only an instant, listening. He could hear the men's voices. He'd stand and fight them, given no other choice. As a rifle barked somewhere behind him, the wounded bruin continued his panicked retreat.

The moment the intruder had waited for came at last. The boys stood still, twin brothers side by side. He put the steel-gray Winchester to his shoulder, firmly gripping the rifle with both hands. He enjoyed the coldness of the barrel, the slick feel of the smooth walnut stock, the intoxicating smell of fresh gun oil. It made him feel powerful, like he was in total control. Nobody could interfere with him now. Laugh, would they? He'd show them. His scarred personality, overflowing with lust and emotion for revenge took over.

With precision accuracy, the steel projectile sliced the air with the lethal speed of a laser beam. Dispatched with deep hostility, the bullet flew on target to it's star-crossed victim. Once again the hawk shuddered his glistening feathers, reacting to the ominous blast.

A millisecond after the rifle report, John heard a thunk that sounded like a lead bullet penetrating a watermelon. In shocked horror he watched as William slumped to the ground, lifeless as last winter's fallen leaves. Replayed as if in slow motion, the screaming hot chunk of lead accurately pierced William's chest cavity scattering chards of flesh and bone, some of which splashed onto his brother's jacket. The bullet ripped his heart into stringy threads of dark red tissue, ending his young life after one final beat. A gaping bloody wound in the twin's back marked the projectile's exit path where it had shredded his shirt and severed his suspenders.

The sinister killer on the near ridge, not pausing to assess the lethal destruction he had caused, quickly jacked another murderous cartridge into the Winchester's firing chamber. A heinous sneer twisted around the corners of his thin lips, 'got to get the other one before he gets away.'

Within a split-second, before he had time to realize the enormity of what had happened, John was puzzled to find himself sprawled on the damp ground. He'd heard the second shot. If it had been intended for him, maybe the bullet had missed. But why was he down? Then he sensed a numbness in his paralyzed right arm. Reaching his usable hand to his shoulder wound he was terrified as he felt the mushy mass of shattered flesh and the warm, sticky flow of blood gushing from beneath his jacket.

John's instinctive reaction was to stand upright. Like a newborn calf he struggled to raise himself on shaky legs, trying to comprehend what was happening. Careful now, mustn't step on William resting there.

Damn, the intruder thought, guess I just winged him. The metallic click of the rifle's loading action kicked a still- smoking empty onto the mossy forest floor and rammed a live cartridge into the breech. The sun became brighter. The diabolical gunman pushed his black hat lower to shade his savage eyes. "Can't let him regain his feet," he muttered.

A momentary glare of sunlight reflected off the gun's shiny steel and lasered across the landscape. The solitary hawk saw the ray but paid no attention. He didn't equate it to breakfast.

As he strained to stand up, young John's eyes darted to the brilliant flash of light reflected from the rifle. And then he saw him. He recognized the killer. "Oh no, William," he gasped to his dead brother. "Oh, God, it's......" Before he could tumble the words from his mouth, a smashing bullet tore into his chest closing his lips forever. He collapsed across William's inert form, sinking into an eternal blackness. Twins in life, the boys were now joined in death.

From the ridge above the carnage the skulking killer surveyed the gruesome scene his ruthless frenzy had inflicted on the quiet countryside. Now, a hush descended on the land and there was an aura of finality in the autumn air.

A sudden movement high in the morning sky caught the killer's attention. A red-tail hawk screeched as it slowly glided off on a drifting thermal. For just a moment the raptor's shrill cry continued to hang in the breeze and then with suddenness it became silent. Deathly still.

Various thoughts raced through the killer's mind as he stood surveying the murder scene. His primary concern was to avoid apprehension, to throw suspicion on others, to apply his cunning by erasing any connection between himself and the murders. He knew he must bury the bodies. Any fool knew that.

In a matter of minutes the crafty killer picked his way through the waist-high brush to where the bodies lay. He was now face-to-face with his gory triumph. The unmistakable smell of death was all around him, hanging like a bitter pall. He relished the obnoxious odor filling his nostrils, a grim reminder of the havoc he had created. His twisted psyche fed as a hungry animal on the butchery strewn before him.

The killer's homicidal disposition was satisfied by the grisly sight of violent death. The thick, sticky blood that had flowed from the twins' bodies onto the damp ground beneath the low-growing salal brush had begun to congeal. It became crusty around the edges of the splotchy puddles. Although he lacked remorse, still he avoided looking at the boys' features, avoided the contorted stare on their ashen faces.

He knew he had work to do. Looking around he saw a broken spruce limb, a casualty of the logger's destructive march through the green timber. A perfect digging tool, he thought.

Leaning his rifle against a gnarled, gray stump he chose an open place of brown clay and began digging the first grave. It wasn't easy. In a few minutes he took off his jacket and hat, laying them in a neat pile beside his gun. The exertion formed small beads of perspiration on his brow and darkened his shirt beneath the arms.

As he paused to catch his breath and wipe his forehead with a red bandana, the killer examined the grave. Not as deep as I'd like, he thought to himself, but probably good enough. He was surprised at the weight of William's body as he dragged it over and dropped it into the shallow depression he had dug. The killer felt something warm and sticky on his fingers; blood. He kicked and shoveled the loose clay onto the body, finally covering all traces of the burial with a stack of dead tree branches.

In less than an hour he had finished the grueling task of burying both boys. Donning jacket and hat, the murderer picked up his rifle, took a last satisfied look at his self-made site of interment and re-traced his path up the hill. He had completed his mission, just as planned—a horrible, bloody mission—an act of revenge and violence.

* * *

The sun was low to the towering western ridge above the burbling waters of the Satsop River when Minnie began fixing supper on the huge, blackened cookstove in the Bauer kitchen. I'd best fix plenty, she thought, they'll be hungry as horses when they come in. The boys will be back from their huntin' trip and Henry's been diggin' spuds all day. She shoved another stick of seasoned alderwood into the firebox. The already hot blaze spat embers and puffs of smoke at her calloused hand. The braised beef in the iron skillet sent a delicious aroma throughout the farmhouse. Minnie had combined the browned meat with a huge kettle of her garden vegetables to make a hearty stew.

Soon she recognized a clumping noise on the porch as someone stomped dirt off their shoes before coming in. Henry shuffled into the kitchen. He hung his jacket on a wooden wall peg, and put his Winchester in the gun rack. "I should have asked the boys to help me today," he said in his deep German accent. "Surely do have a lotta diggin' to do."

"They ain't back from huntin' yet," Minnie said as she stirred the stew with a long wooden spoon.

"Maybe they got somethin' and it's takin' 'em awhile." he replied, slumping into a chair like a limp sack of rags. "I heard some shootin' earlier, could have been them, sounded like it was towards the river. Supper ready yet?"

"Why don't we wait a spell?" Minnie suggested. "It's near ready but maybe they'll come draggin' in soon."

"Well o.k. but I'm powerful hungry."

"What's that stain on your trousers?" Minnie asked.

Glancing down at his pant leg, Henry replied, "Ain't nothin', I surprised a raccoon in the spud patch. Hit him with my shovel, sure did bleed all over everythin'."

Twilight began to settle over the Satsop country and Minnie worried when the twins still hadn't returned home. As the black night swallowed up the last rays of the sun over the western sky, Henry said, "Let's eat, they'll probably show up about the time we sit down."

After dinner, Minnie cleared the table and put the stew pot on the back of the stove to keep it warm. She told her husband, "I'm really gettin' worried. They never been this late for supper before, it's near nine o' clock."

"I'll take a lantern and go look for them but sure as shootin' I'll probably meet 'em soon's I get past the barn."

"Well I'll feel better about it if we're at least tryin' to find 'em," Minnie said, out of nervousness toying with her gold wedding band.

With a deep sigh that Minnie thought sounded sarcastic, Henry put on his hat and jacket, grabbed his rifle off the wall rack, and lit a kerosene lantern, slamming the door as he went out. For the next hour she paced the parlor's uneven wood floor like a caged animal. On occasion she went to the front window, peering into the blackness for any glimmer of hope that John and William were coming home.

Two hours passed. Just before midnight Minnie leaped from her chair like an uncoiled spring when she heard a noise on the porch. Rushing to the door she jerked it open. Lantern hanging loosely at his side, a bedraggled husband announced, "Didn't find nothin', Min, and I went all the way to the river, then to the top of the ridge. Can't figure where they might have gone. Can't figure it at all. Only thing that makes any sense, they must have got lost and decided to hole up for the night. Smart thing to do."

Minnie's voice became high-pitched and trembled. "What are we gonna do, Henry?"

He knew she'd been crying. He could see the streaks of tears on her cheeks reflected in the lantern light. "Don't get yourself all worked up. If they don't show up by mornin' I'll ride into Matlock and call the sheriff. They're more n' likely just lost. He can bring a posse and help look for them."

The parents spent a sleepless night and rolled out of bed early the next morning. After breakfast Henry hitched the mare to the buggy and drove to Matlock where he phoned Sheriff Ed Payette. "My two boys went huntin' and ain't come back yet," the German homesteader told him in his broken dialect. "They're like as not just lost in the woods but we need your help to find 'em."

At once Payette dispatched Deputies Colin McKenzie and Carl

Swartz with instructions, "Stop and see if Ed Maas will let you use his bloodhounds to track them boys."

Nothing moved fast in 1911. Especially in the backwoods country of western Washington State. The two deputies drove a team and wagon over rutted country roads dotted with axle-busting mudholes to reach the Bauer homestead. Enroute they stopped at the Ed Maas place and asked about his hounds.

"Sure, I'll take the dogs and go along. Give me a couple minutes to gather up a few things. The dogs don't need no coaxin'. They're always rarin' to go," Maas said, grinning. It was nearly four o'clock in the afternoon when McKenzie wheeled the wagon into the Bauer front yard. Henry and Minnie had heard them coming and met the posse and Maas on the porch.

"Any sign of 'em yet?" Swartz yelled to the parents as he swung down from the wooden wagon's high spring seat. He knew the answer before Minnie shook her head no.

"We're grateful you've come," Henry said, walking across the damp yard to meet them. "They's been gone more than twenty-four

One entire section of the museum is devoted to pictures and artifacts from the Tornow episodes.

hours and their ma's gettin' plenty worried."

"We just want our boys home," Minnie sobbed, her lack of sleep evident by the deep wrinkles in her sunken cheeks and dark circles under her eyes.

"Don't fret Mrs. Bauer," Ed Maas said in a reassuring tone. "These hounds are real good at trackin' people. You got a piece of clothing they can get a scent from?"

As Henry threw one of John's old caps on the ground, the hounds rushed to it in a frenzy, sniffing like they were smelling out a bear. Eager for the hunt the two dogs strained on their leather leashes almost pulling Maas off balance.

"We've still got a few hours of daylight, let's see what the dogs might come up with," McKenzie suggested. With Maas and the liver-brown hounds leading the way, McKenzie, Swartz, and the German father began tracking on a cattle trail through beds of creeping, yellow buttercups behind the barn.

"This is like as not where they started out," Henry told the deputies. Mournful baying and excited woof-woofing from the dogs confirmed they were on the right trail.

"We're onto 'em," the dog's handler said, recognizing his hounds' increased level of excitement. "Hope the scent holds for them, we had a fair to middlin' rain last night, you know."

The tracking dogs ran arrow-straight for awhile across the open, logged off, elevated plain. Soon they sat down and looked dejectedly at their owner with their round, soulful eyes. "Rain must have washed out the scent," he said. "Let's circle the dogs around this spot to see if we can pick up a trail."

This time-consuming procedure was tried again and again. The hounds would have a hot trail for awhile, then lose it, run again, then lose the scent.

They'd been following a narrow dirt trail the range cattle used to get to the river. Like a flat ribbon the path meandered through the varied landscape: now open and flat, next a valley of green cascara and alder trees, soon a field of ghost-like gray stumps. Higher on the ridge there was a small patch of bypassed Douglas fir timber, with salal and red huckleberry growing in sporadic plots. It was typical logged-off country where the remaining trees were mostly junk species unwanted by the mills, or vine maples and a few alders here and there.

Heavy, dark clouds began moving in from the southwest, threatening rain and hurrying nightfall. Deputy McKenzie cast a wary eye at the gathering shadows like a ship's captain would try to outguess a storm. "It don't look none too good," he told the others as they rested on a couple of blown down alders. "No sir, it don't look good at all."

"Gettin' dark too," Deputy Swartz said. "Best we get out of here before we get lost ourselves."

By the time the posse returned to the Bauer homestead, darkness had settled like a heavy black shroud over the Olympic foothills. The hounds were quiet now, having worked out their excitement on the trail. The men weren't saying much either.

Leaving Henry on the porch, McKenzie said, "We'll go down and stay with Ed tonight. Be back tomorrow at first light."

Tell your Missus not to fret. With a full day tomorrow we should find your boys."

"Thanks for your help," Henry said, pulling off his wet and dirty boots on the wooden front porch.

In soggy stocking feet Henry clumped into the house, dreading to tell his wife they'd found nothing. "Well, maybe tomorrow," he concluded, sharing the bad news. "Maybe tomorrow we'll find 'em." Yet his voice lacked the optimism Minnie needed to reassure the diminishing hope she felt for her sons. She needed that hope like a shipwrecked victim needs a life ring. Minnie needed that hope in her sea of despair.

It had been a long and grueling day for the Bauer parents. Laying in bed that night, Henry was stretched out flat on his back like a corpse in a coffin. He always snored on his back. Minnie was awake like it was noon instead of midnight. Partly due to her husband's sonorous breathing, partly because of the worry over her missing sons. Then she heard it. Faint at first but at intervals a louder noise. She was concerned but didn't want to wake her husband. He wouldn't wake up if the roof fell in, she thought.

Quietly she slipped out of bed, into her slippers and old patched robe she'd had since a teenager. Now Minnie could see dancing shafts of light from a swinging lantern in the down- stairs kitchen, accompanied by rustling and scraping sounds like somebody was raiding her pantry. Who could it be at this time of night? Wide awake now, she tiptoed down towards the bobbing lantern light, her heart pounding in apprehension.

Minnie remembered her mother's cane hanging on a peg in the lower hallway. Trembling, without making a sound, she grabbed it. Not much of a weapon against intruders but better than nothing. From the upstairs bedroom she continued to hear Henry's full-throated snoring.

Weapon at the ready, Minnie stood cloaked by the darkness, peering around the corner, trying to identify the intruder. The kitchen's back door was wide open, explaining how he had entered. She saw him moving around, silhouetted by lantern light, moving as if looking for something in the cupboards.

As she recognized him she uttered a tiny muted squeal of delight. "John, Baby Brother, what are you doing here at this time of night?" Minnie whispered.

"Hi Sis," John said in a low voice. "Sorry to have woke you up, just stopped by for some grub to take with me when I go back out to the hills."

"Oh John," she said in a weepy little voice, "the twins are missing, ain't been home for two nights. They went huntin' and we ain't seen 'em since."

John paused, staring at Minnie with a look of concern. "Seems unusual, but I wouldn't fret too much. They probably shot a bear or somethin' and are havin' a tough time gettin' it out of the woods. These things happen quite regular."

"Oh I hope you're right," Minnie whispered, not to wake Henry.

John continued gathering foodstuffs; a sack of salt, a part bag of flour, half a tin of coffee, a loaf of fresh bread. "You don't mind me takin' these things, do you Min?" he asked, putting the items in his packsack.

"Course not, help yourself. Take some of those cookies in the bread box I just baked."

"I'm headin' for the high country Sis, but I'll meander a bit to see if I can find William and John. It's a big country, they could be anyplace, but I'm sure they're all right."

"If anyone can find 'em, you can," Minnie said, a hopeful look on her tired face.

"I ain't comin' back for quite a spell. Got no use for town folks no more. Not my brother Ed, neither. I've had my fill of him after he shot Cougar. If it wasn't for you and the boys I'd never come back," John concluded as he gave his sister a peck on the cheek. He blew out the lantern, eased out the door without a sound, and melted into the darkness like just another shadow.

Watching him leave she said, "I'll miss you Baby Brother, surely I will."

* * *

The Bauers were already up and eating breakfast the next morning when they heard the pounding hooves, clattering wagon and baying hounds in the yard. Swallowing his last bite of oatmeal, Henry went out on the porch. He was shirtless except for his longjohn top, which he seldom took off, and suspenders hanging to his knees. "Come in and have a cup of coffee," he called to them, in his guttural German accent.

Studying the weather, Henry noted first light was just dawning in the cloudless sky while fading stars glimmered in the morning chillness. All around, the grass and bushes were slickened from the evening's moisture. Out front, beyond the wagon, leaves on the big-leaf maple trees were yellowing, portraying nature's calendar, turning golden reds and yellows with the advent of fall.

The posse members trooped in while Minnie grabbed every cup she owned to serve them coffee. Scurrying to the table, Minnie passed full mugs of steaming hot brew, asking, "Can I get you anything to eat? How about some cookies I just baked?" she suggested, going to the bread box. "Oh dear, they're just about gone."

"I phoned the sheriff last night from down at Ed's place," Deputy McKenzie said. "He told me he'd try to get some more men up here. We've got to find those boys today."

"We will, Colin," Henry said, "I'm sure we will."

The hounds were eager as pups on a rabbit chase. They'd been tied to a wagon wheel with their heavy leather leashes. When they saw the men coming from the house, the dogs raised a ruckus with their baying and barking. Their excited breath spewed mini-clouds of steam into the cold morning air.

Henry unharnessed the visitor's team and put them to pasture with his own horses.

Ed Maas handled the dogs, Deputies McKenzie and Swartz carried rifles and were close behind. Henry was last as the posse hit the trail behind the barn. Minnie could hear the hounds yowling long

Rand Iversen simulates a call on an old-time telephone similar to the one used by Giles Quimby in April, 1913, to alert Sheriff Mathews of the shootout at Tornow Lake.

after they were out of sight. She peered out the window at the fluffy, white clouds drifting in over the southeastern hills. The sky gave promise of a rainless day as the sun cast an occasional long shadow through the now broken overcast. She momentarily clasped her roughened hands to her bosom in prayer for the safe return of her sons, for good weather so the hounds could track, for the safety of everyone in the posse.

In about an hour, just past the farthest point they'd gone the day before, the hounds began to sing their familiar sound of success. "They're onto something," Maas said. "It's all I can do to hold 'em but I don't dare let 'em loose. Here, Carl, you take one, help me out."

With the deputy holding back on a straining, baying bloodhound, the dogs led the posse towards the river. Noses to the ground, the hounds veered off the trail following a cross-country path of tromped down green thimbleberry brush.

Pausing to examine the trail, McKenzie said, "Hey boys, I think the dogs are trackin' a bear, a wounded bear at that. See them tracks? And look here at the fresh drops of blood."

The others gathered around him to look for themselves. "You're right," Ed Maas said, "maybe the twins wounded him."

As they continued, the pace was slowed by the dense underbrush, barbed Himalayan blackberry vines and blown-down trees, some more than four feet in diameter. In just a few minutes they halted at the crystal-clear waters of the Satsop River. The dogs eagerly waded into the shallow stream, lapping up the cold, sparkling water like they hadn't drunk in a week.

Getting down on all fours, McKenzie closely inspected the trail that had disappeared into the river. Like a bloodhound himself, he lowered his head and sniffed the tracks. "Phew," he uttered, "that's a bear all right. Looks like he crossed the river through these low willows."

"You can smell those tracks?" Henry asked, wide-eyed and incredulous.

"Sure, if they're fresh enough and if you don't use tobacco," McKenzie said, straightening up and brushing the wet gravel from his trouser knees.

The posse waded across the river and the hounds again picked up the trail. Resuming their baying and woofing eagerness, they strained on their leashes to follow the bear's tracks.

* * *

He heard them coming. He'd heard them for quite awhile but hoped maybe they wouldn't bother him. He needed a rest. The pain in his side had worsened. It had become a hot, throbbing pain, nearly paralyzing his hind legs. The bear suddenly thrust his muzzle skywards, testing the air, trying to identify his pursuers. As he caught the scent, a jolt of fear rippled through his sinewy body—

dogs—his hated enemies.

With agony in every faltering movement, he got onto his feet and turned his glistening black head towards the sound of the approaching posse. It was decision time. He could run no farther. The wound had drained all his stamina. He could climb a nearby fir tree—if he had the strength for it—or he could stand and fight. Fight these hated dogs and the equally hated men. Disregarding the excruciating pain the bear stood up on his hind legs in the dense underbrush, standing erect to his almost six foot height, ready to fight for his life.

"Look up there," McKenzie shouted, "there's the bear. Hold them dogs. Old Blackie will rip 'em to pieces."

The men had an awesome advantage, an unfair superiority. It wasn't much of a fight.

"I'll take him," McKenzie yelled, throwing his rifle to his shoulder. The single shot found it's easy target. The bear crumpled into a forlorn pile of shiny black hair.

The posse returned to the river where they rested and ate sandwiches they'd carried in deep jacket pockets. Ed Maas was the first to speak, "Henry's twins probably wounded that bear. If we backtrack we should be able to pick up their trail."

"Makes sense to me," the German homesteader said as he poked his index finger at pieces of sandwich stuck to his teeth. Following lunch the men split up so they could cover more territory. It was tough going through the jungle-like brush. Difficult for the men but easy for the dogs who were built low to the ground. They crawled under the worst entanglements.

They crisscrossed the hills, valleys and flatlands where the bear had been. Nothing. Thinking they might have missed something they covered the same terrain again. Still nothing.

At mid-afternoon they rested on a small flat area between two valleys. Colin McKenzie climbed onto a low, gnarled gray stump, removed his sweat-stained hat and wiped his brow with his red bandana. "We should have seen some sign of the boys by now," he said. "I can't understand this. The rain must have washed out the scent."

"Brush is awful thick," Ed Maas said, lighting his pipe, puffing billowing clouds of smoke that drifted across the flat. "If they ain't alive they could be anywhere in this damned rough country."

McKenzie gazed at the hillsides, the lush green valleys, the patch of timber on the ridge above them. What are we overlooking, he thought, gazing upward. He watched fleecy white clouds drifting about in the pleasant autumn sky. Closer now, he looked at the stumps and debris left in the wake of the bygone logging operation, chunks of discarded logs, piles of dead tree branches. Suddenly his eyes darted back to the stacks of branches. Wait a minute, he thought, why are those limbs all in a pile? Loggers spread their debris, they don't pile it up so neat.

Sliding off his gnarled stump with a questioning glance the deputy casually walked over to have a closer look at the pile of tree branches. Then he saw it. The fresh digging in the dirt beneath the pile. Bending down on one knee he picked up a handful of the loose clay. Next he thrust his hand into the soft dirt. He felt something solid. McKenzie recognized the feel of what he'd found. A human hand. "Oh, God, no," the deputy uttered, hanging his head as if in prayer.

Watching him, Carl Swartz asked, "Whatcha got Colin? Did you find something?"

Saying nothing McKenzie got up, shaking the dirt from his hand and slowly walked over to Henry Bauer, putting an arm around him. "I'm terrible sorry Henry. I think I've found your boys."

The men pulled the logging debris off the grave and digging with the same stubby limb used by the killer, uncovered the body of John Bauer. He had been shot twice, once in the shoulder and the fatal shot to his chest. In dour silence, the German father helped unearth

134

the body of his son.

"What's that over there?" Ed Maas questioned, pointing to a second pile of suspicious looking brush.

In just a few minutes they found the body of William Bauer who had been killed instantly by a bullet through his heart.

It was now getting late in the afternoon. The posse covered the bodies with squares of canvas, leaving them to be examined by the coroner the next day.

Returning crestfallen to the Bauer homestead, the posse was met by Sheriff Ed Payette and two deputies. McKenzie gave Payette the bad news while Henry, head hanging in dejection, went inside to break the sorrowful events to Minnie.

* * *

With Payette's call to Coroner R.F. Hunter from the Maas place, word of the twins' murder spread like wildfire.

The next day McKenzie led the Sheriff, an investigative posse and Coroner Hunter to the grisly crime scene. On the way in, the deputy told Sheriff Payette, "While we were searching, we came across a lean-to camp that Henry Bauer said looked to him like it had been used by that wild fellow, John Tornow. He wasn't there but it looked like he had used the lean-to not very long ago."

"Tornow's brother came into the office just last month, his name was Edward as I recall," Payette said. "He tried to swear out a warrant for his brother, John. Seemed to me like a family squabble but now I'd be interested in talking with this fellow who spends most of his time living in the woods," the Sheriff concluded. The disheartened posse tramped single-file towards the murder scene.

Turning to Deputy McKenzie who was walking behind him, Payette asked, "You've been there, Colin, what do you think happened?"

"Hard to say Ed, several fellows might become suspects. John

Tornow might have been in the lean-to, heard the boys shooting at the bear, thought someone was shooting at him, and returned the fire. We saw where some meat had been dry-jerkied."

"But I've heard tell he thought the world of his nephews," the Sheriff answered. "How about one of the family members? They say John is due to inherit quite a chunk of money from his parents' estate. If he wasn't around the dough would go to the surviving relatives. Someone might be trying to frame John for this murder, you know what I mean?"

In awhile the posse stopped at a small creek for a drink and a short rest.

Deputy Schwartz said, "Some folks say John Tornow's demented but I've talked with others who know him and they say he's just shy around people. And I'm wonderin' myself about this Kennedy guy who's been seen around the Bauer place. Did you hear that Henry Bauer ran Kennedy off his property?"

"Talkin' about that I hate to mention it but old man Bauer himself could become a suspect," McKenzie said as they got up to continue their journey. "I've heard he has a terrible temper and has always feuded with his in-laws, the Tornows."

Continuing along the trail, Schwartz mentioned, "I don't think John was all that jiggled in the head. They say he never makes camp near running water. The noise could drown out the sound of someone trying to sneak up on him. Demented? Yeah, crazy like a fox."

Coroner Hunter had been quiet, listening to the various theories as they marched along the narrow trail through the brushy Satsop country. Now he spoke, telling the sheriff, "Sounds like you've got a plentiful supply of suspects, Ed. Maybe when I examine the bodies I can narrow it down for you. Maybe not. We seem to have two victims killed by a high-powered rifle. Direction of bullet path might be all the help I'll be able to give you."

As they continued down the trail Payette thought about the case and weighed different options in his mind. He knew there could be several suspects but he was leaning almost 100 percent towards the theory that John Tornow had killed the boys. He wanted very much to question John but realized that wouldn't be easy. Payette knew that finding the loner would be difficult.

The posse carried the bodies out to the Bauer homestead. From there they were taken to the mortuary in Montesano. Through tear-filled eyes, Minnie viewed her sons as they lay quiet and peaceful in the back of the wagon.

Henry Bauer took Sheriff Payette aside, telling him, "Whoever done this took the jackets and some personal effects from my boys."

The next day the sheriff petitioned the commissioners to put up a $500 reward for the apprehension of John Tornow for questioning in the Bauer boys' killing. He also launched a full-scale manhunt into the rugged Olympic Mountain foothills for John, mustering a posse of up to a dozen expert woodsmen.

* * *

About a week after the murders, timber cruisers Mike Scully and Earl McIntosh were relaxing around their campfire one evening, deep in the wild Olympic country. As Scully finished washing their tin plates, McIntosh threw a dry length of hemlock onto the fire. It knocked embers and smoke into the cool darkness around their temporary camp.

Out of nowhere, without warning, a straggly six foot tall figure appeared at the edge of the firelight, holding a rifle across folded arms. He just emerged from the darkness, like an apparition from the gloomy black night. "What are you fellows doin' in here?" John Tornow asked, a deep scowl creasing his bearded face.

Surprised and shaken, pale as chalk, the cruisers stood up to greet their menacing visitor. "We're just out here tallying timber for

Giles Quimby, credited with ending the reign of John Tornow as he appeared in his uniform during the Spanish-American War.

Simpson," Scully explained. "Who are you?"

"Name's John. John Tornow. Maybe you've heard 'bout me. I'm out here a lot."

"We just finished supper but there's some beans and salt pork left if you're hungry," McIntosh offered.

"Thanks," John said, "that sounds good." He laid his rifle on a large rock and sat beside the fire on his haunches as the cruiser filled a plate for him.

Just a bit hesitant, Skully asked, "Did you know the Bauer boys have been murdered?"

John's fork paused halfway to his mouth. "Oh my God! No, I didn't know that. Who done it?"

The cruisers looked with uncertainty at each other, neither feeling comfortable to tell John he was the prime suspect. At last, Scully broke the silence with slow, chopped words. "John, they seem to think you did it. Now me and Earl we don't think you did but the law is out looking for you."

Putting down the plate of beans, John's face became flushed. His obvious anger showed even in the dim fire light. The cruisers were glad John's rifle was several steps away.

"What's the matter with them?" he shouted in anger as the muscles in his neck tightened like steel cables. "I wouldn't harm them boys. They was my nephews. I loved them. Sis told me they'd gone huntin' and got lost. I been lookin' for them myself of late. Figured they just as not made it home by now."

Rolling a cigarette between his fingers, Scully said, "They found the bodies just a mile or so from the homestead." Then he lit the Bull Durham smoke, hoping it would help settle his nerves.

The pair watched with apprehension as John walked over and picked up his rifle. "You tell everyone I didn't do it. They can try to come after me. Just let 'em, I ain't never goin' back again. Never on your life." And with that declaration, John melted away into the ring of darkness just outside the campfire's halo of light. Disappeared as if he'd stepped off the face of the earth.

Chapter Six

RAT-A-TAT-TAT, RAT-A-TAT-TAT, WAS IT A MACHINE GUN? WHO WOULD be out in this wilderness with an automatic gun? No roads, no ranches, hardly a living soul. John heard it again. He smiled, recognizing the sound.

Rifle at hand, in silence he prowled through waist-high, erect clumps of dark-green sword ferns still wet from the morning dew. His trained eyes searched the lofty forest canopy for the source of the staccato hammering. There, he heard it again, closer this time. It was a pure outdoors sound. He enjoyed it, wanted to locate it, then just sit and listen, filling his head with the repetitive rattling noise.

A lofty western red cedar snag poked it's weathered spire above the tallest firs, it's gray, hollow shell still upright despite the conifer's death a long while ago. The busy culprit was visible, tenaciously clinging to the upper reaches of the tree's softened wood trunk. *Rat-a-tat-tat* he went again in his boldness, demonstrating to the man intruder he wasn't afraid of him. The spotted-breast sapsucker sounded like a jackhammer working on an empty oil barrel. The feisty little driller stopped his hammering search for insects to sound a defiant trill, a slurred, "cherr" at John.

"Go ahead, keep bangin' your beak against that old tree," John said, a satisfied smile creeping across his darkened features. "I'll just sit here quietlike and watch." As if in answer, *rat-a-tat-tat* went the sapsucker, drilling his hole deeper into the rotten wood.

As John sat amidst the pristine wilderness his aimless thoughts darted like a skitter bug on a glassy lake. The faint, small voice from within his head intensified his insecurity, his feelings of guilt, his doubts about what may have occurred. *Maybe you killed your nephews without knowin' it,* the determined little gremlin in his subconscious nagged him like a guilty conscience.

"No, no, I wouldn't of killed 'em," the forest loner pleaded aloud. "They was my sister's boys. I loved 'em both."

But this avowed denial heightened his uncertainty and compounded his buildup of stress. Casting his gaze away from the ever-hammering sapsucker, John dropped his head between his outdoor-roughened palms, exclaiming, "Leave me alone, why do you keep eatin' away at me? You're gonna drive me crazy." Some would later say it may have already happened.

* * *

Longtime Satsop valley cattle rancher, Joseph Carstairs sat on the porch bench at the Matlock General Store one Indian summer afternoon in 1911 watching the horse-drawn buggies and occasional motor car putter by.

It was a tiny hamlet; a few bare-board houses, the hotel converted into a boarding house yet still had lots of vacancies, the shoemaker left town months ago with a logger's wife. The place had an illusion of Hooterville.

Down the narrow, dirt street, Carstairs saw a billowing cloud of dust following a shiny green Reo automobile. Coming towards him on that warm afternoon, it shattered his sun worshiping.

The showy car pulled up at the store and parked between two buggies whose horses were tied to the hitching rail. The driver smiled, turned off the ignition switch. The resultant backfire startled the two horses and made them shy sideways with a fearful whinny.

"Hi there, Kennedy," Carstairs greeted the impeccably dressed owner of the flashy car. "I see you've got yourself a new automobile."

"Yes," Kennedy replied, stepping with a flourish off the car's running board. "It's a 1911 Reo, first one in Matlock, first one in the county for that matter," a touch of boastfulness in his voice.

"Sure scares the horses," the affirmed rancher shot back at him. He knew full well in his own mind that gasoline autos were just a flash in the pan, destined for the scrap heap when owners realized the new-fangled things weren't as reliable as horses.

Before sitting down beside Carstairs, Kennedy first wiped the bench with a stark-white linen handkerchief. "Did you hear about the Bauer boys being murdered last week?" Kennedy asked.

"Yes I did. What kind of a deranged person would do such a thing?"

"Well, some are saying the ornery German father was somewhat to blame because of the way he treated the boys and his wife," Kennedy said, with a subtle raise of his eyebrows.

"Ain't got nothing to do with it," Carstairs declared, looking Kennedy straight-on and loading up the crusty bowl of his battered pipe with stringy tobacco from a well-worn leather pouch.

"I think Tornow did it," Kennedy said, playing devil's advocate and oozing self-confidence.

"John or Edward?" Carstairs inquired, touching a flaming wooden match to the blackened pipe held tight-lipped in his firm jaw.

"Why John, of course. Everyone knows he's demented," Kennedy smiled, to test the rancher's opinion.

"The lad has worked for me off and on down through the years," the rancher replied. "I never saw nothing wrong with his head. But I'm not so sure about the other brother. That fellow is a different story."

"Well, maybe," Kennedy grunted in feigned disagreement. "Been good talking with you, I've got to get along now, got to buy some ammunition and gun oil."

* * *

The funeral for John and William Bauer was attended by almost everyone in the Satsop-Matlock area, everyone except John Tornow who was being sought for questioning by the law. Following the services Minnie sank into a deep depression; mourning for her dead sons, not believing her brother was guilty of the crime—but at the same time being uncertain about who had killed them, and trying to close her mind to negative thinking about her husband...terrible thoughts...quite frightening thoughts.

Henry just became more ornery. When he pulled his dull-gold watch out of his pocket by it's blackened leather thong and supper wasn't on the table precisely at six, he bellowed like a bull penned away from the heifers. "Get your mind off your troubles and heed your duties," he yelled at her. "Quit cryin' over spilt milk. What's done is done."

When things were at their worst, Minnie wished she'd learned how to shoot a rifle. Henry's rifle was always hanging on the kitchen wall. Maybe it wasn't too late to learn, she thought to herself bitterly. Maybe not.

* * *

Even during the late 1800's little was known about the interior of the rugged mountains on western Washington's Olympic Peninsula. The early Indians believed the Olympics were inhabited by evil spirits—the thunderbirds—who on occasion demonstrated their supernatural talents by exploding frightful lightning storms of dazzling pyrotechnic proportions above 8,000-foot Mt. Olympus. Flatland farmers never wandered in. Crusty old homesteader Fred Winkleman was heard to mutter, "Ain't got no use for them mountains; too rocky to plow, too steep for pasture."

In 1889-1890, a Seattle newspaper bankrolled the first expedition through the rugged wilderness. Soon afterward a military expedition led by Lieutenant Joseph O'Neil demonstrated considerable bravery by plunging into the unknown country. These two explorations disproved a legend the Olympics were home to a magical garden of Eden, with a unique array of exotic plants and animals.

Towards this mountainous no-man's-land, John Tornow fled. Within it's 6,000 square-miles of craggy wilderness, he could become insignificant as a grain of sand on a mile-long beach. He could be even more difficult to find than the proverbial needle in a haystack.

John trekked farther and farther into the bowels of this wild outback country. First, ten miles from the home place; then fifteen; sometimes twenty or twenty-five. He decided to move farther back; he might find a new area of seclusion; a place where people would leave him alone. Deep in the mountains, he could become content and fulfilled; one with the forest, the animals, the tranquility. The loner carried his memories—good memories, a storehouse of his mind about those he loved—nightmares, the frightening events inflicted by people who disliked or misunderstood him.

* * *

After the gruesome murders of the Bauer twins, a cry of vengeance surged from many urbanites in the county—*get Tornow!* But most of the Tornow friends and neighbors in the upper Satsop valley—those who knew John best—were not convinced of his guilt. They urged caution and fairness, demanded more proof. Circumstantial evidence was too thin; insufficient to convict a man before he'd been questioned.

Historical researchers found not a single report of any suspects ever having been investigated by lawmen for the Bauer murders. John's guilt had been established on flimsy circumstantial information. Disregarding other valid motives and clues, officers focused on one hapless loner. Whether he was innocent or guilty, this prejudiced accusation transformed John Tornow into a hunted fugitive. His only proven transgression had been an insatiable love for the outdoors and a strong desire to abstain from a society that he felt had been inhospitable.

* * *

During October of 1911, the Olympic foothills were tramped by several posses dispatched by Sheriff Payette. The rugged wilderness saw more visitors than ever before as searchers combed the country for John Tornow. It was difficult, dangerous and frightening. Posse members knew John was aware of their presence. George Stormes would later tell how he felt:

"We traipsed the valleys and hillsides, mostly in deep virgin timber because the logging companies hadn't been that far back yet. It was nervous work, let me tell you. We knew Tornow could be hiding behind any tree or boulder. We figured he probably kept tabs on us. We followed old elk trails and sometimes we'd come across human tracks that could have been his. As we went pussyfooting along on the trails, we'd all of a sudden stop. Here we were, following him. But we had a spooky kind of feeling that he was also following us. Jeez, it made the hair on my neck stand straight up. You just knew he was there watching us, waiting, doubtless could have drilled any of us whenever he wanted to."

* * *

There was a profound feeling of fall in the crisp, frosty mornings; the aroma of dried leaves and fallen pine cones, the noticeable clues of changing seasons as nature tucked away the summer's prolific growth and greenery as if to protect the wilderness from the coming cold season. When autumn began deferring to early winter, hillsides became alive with vivid hues of gold and crimson deciduous leaves, just like an old master's heavy tinged oil painting.

The chill in the air also reminded John Tornow he needed to prepare for the coming of harsh weather. As the squirrels stashed away stockpiles of seed cones, John realized he'd need a food supply for the long, cold winter. Risking disclosure of his location, he knew he must shoot an elk and smoke the meat to fill his larders in several well-concealed hideouts.

Early one November day, black, moisture-filled, Chinook storm clouds rolled in over the craggy peaks of the Olympics, colliding with updrafts of cooler air from the valley floor. The swirling maelstrom produced torrents of rain and in the higher atmosphere the super-energized clouds threw off bolts of jagged lightning that zapped the taller mountains. The resultant strikes sent rolling waves of booming thunder throughout the shadowed countryside, spawning a cataclysmic, roiling tempest. It smelled of ozone and sounded like an artillery duel; as if the storm kings were battling for possession of this corner of the Olympics.

As the dark clouds almost turned day into night, John stepped out of his primitive bark-slab shelter, a murky wildnerness-type shack, much like the fugitive himself. He raised his face skyward. The heavy rain drops pelted his tanned, bearded face. Small rivulets of water ran down his neck. He closed his eyes and opened his mouth, drinking in the torrents unleashed by the thunderstorm. Standing there, laughing like a child at play, his clothing drenched, he thought, thank you Lord for this storm. Now I can shoot me an elk, smoke it over an alder fire, and nobody will see or hear me.

* * *

The rugged northern peaks and glacier-gouged ravines of the lower Olympics were blanketed by the first heavy snowfall in early December. The white mantle was gentle at first; dusting rocky hillsides, turning the forest greenery into shadowy white shrouds—like a sprinkling of powdered sugar. But then, with increased fury, the weather gods suffocated the land with deep drifts that buried everything with bottomless piles of chalky-white snow. Winter had arrived in the mountains. "Send out the word, call the posses in," Sheriff

Payette instructed Deputy Giles Quimby. "Let's call off the search for John Tornow. The bad weather should drive him down to the flatlands and he'll be easier to apprehend for questioning."

So, at the end of 1911, nearly four months after the murder of the Bauer twins, the search for John Tornow, loner turned fugitive, was called off for the winter. The sheriff's prediction was somewhat correct. As the snow piled ever deeper John stepped out of his well-concealed hideout one day and speculated on his situation. His boots squeaked in the new-fallen snow. He sank to his knees in the deep drifts.

Motionless for a moment, John at once noticed something un-usual. An eerie hush of stillness had descended on the forest. The sound absorbent blanket of white quieted the land. Small animals hibernated, as did the bears, tucked away in warm burrows, oblivious to the winter weather. Deer, elk and their predators had moved down to warmer elevations. Gone were the birds to more comfortable climes, all but the most hardy, just those attuned to nature's winter fury remained behind.

John sensed the stillness, the isolation and his inability to move rapidly if necessary. "Alright, I'll leave too," he told the white-capped mountains, arms outstretched in a gesture of appeasement to the weather gods. "But I'm comin' back. Don't you forget it." The sound of his echoing proclamation was muted at once by the deep snow banks. John loaded his packsack and followed the migration trail to the lowlands; down closer to those who would incarcerate him.

* * *

The Matlock dirt roads were greasy-slick from the winter rain and snow as John Kennedy wheeled into the General Store in his not-so-shiny, green Reo one day in February, 1912. The car's exterior was splotched with sticky dried mud. The undercarriage was encased with the hardened clay, as though it had been purposely mummified.

At the explosive backfire, the storekeeper grimaced, knowing full-well who had just arrived. He didn't care much for Kennedy but enjoyed his business. Business was not too brisk right now so he was cordial and accommodating towards the dandy.

"Good morning, Mr. Kennedy," he condescendingly purred in his most syrupy voice. "What can I help you with today?"

"Just stopped by to pick up a bag of quick-lime for the hired man to use in the barn," Kennedy replied, walking to the bin where it was often stocked.

"Oh dear," the store-keep said, "I'm afraid we're out of quick-lime. Mrs. Bauer bought the last we had a couple of weeks ago."

Kennedy stopped in his tracks like he'd just walked into a stone wall. "Mrs. Bauer?" he questioned. "Why would Mrs. Bauer be buying quick-lime? I thought her husband did all the trading."

"Henry Bauer hasn't been in the store for a long spell. I dunno, maybe it's been several months since I last saw him. His Missus does all the trading now. Asked her about him last week, I did, but she just said he was gone somewheres."

"Hmmm. That's very interesting."

"Do you want me to order some quick-lime for you? We can have it come in on the train tomorrow," the clerk asked of the departing Kennedy.

"Sure, that will be fine. No hurry. No hurry at all."

Hastening to his automobile, Kennedy's curiosity was aroused. Does this mean that Minnie is all alone since the twins had been murdered last autumn? At that time he'd wanted to console Minnie but with Henry around he'd thought better of it. He wondered. And where was that damned husband? He pondered, checking the Reo's rear seat to make sure his rifle was there. Also questioning why a woman alone would need quick-lime. Kennedy decided to get answers to his questions, answers that Minnie alone could provide.

He spun the Reo's crank handle. *Uhrawooo, uhrawooo* ground the crankshaft, *clickety-clackety* as the valves sprang to life, *varoom-varoom* sang the auto's engine as Kennedy gave it the gas and wheeled away from the store.

Maneuvering with caution over the narrow muddy road towards the Bauer homestead, Kennedy recalled bygone days when the irate husband had almost thrown him off the front porch. He would be more vigilant now. More careful, unhurried.

Kennedy knew a place on the high ridge where he could observe the Bauer homestead undetected. He parked beside the road and walked through the low-growing dwarf blueberry and common salal brush to the edge of the summit. Soon he came to a large, gray stump about 400 yards above the cabin. Muttering to himself, using a clean handkerchief he wiped the bits of mud from his shiny English leather boots. He would wait, observe the homestead to make certain Henry was gone. He'd take no chances this time on running into the quick-tempered husband. It had been a humiliating experience. He'd learned.

Hours passed. The afternoon sun dropped low on the horizon, casting elongated shadows from split-cedar fence posts onto the Bauer's scrubby pasture. Still no sign of Minnie's husband. Now it was safe.

Stepping into the Reo, Kennedy wiped his boots, adjusted his Italian silk tie and picked off a few dry huckleberry leaves that had attached to his forest-green trousers.

With apprehension he pulled into the muddy Bauer yard, turned off the car's ignition and once again glanced at his rifle. With caution he picked his way towards the porch, stepping on hard dirt clods rather than sticky mud.

Minnie heard something loud as a rifle shot; she ran to the window, peered out—seemed impossible—but there he was, wearing his cashmere jacket, Bristol fashion pressed trousers and a wide smile.

He's come back. After all this time, she thought to herself.

No chance to primp. Oh dear, my hair's a mess. Guess this dress ain't got no spots on it. She threw the door wide open even before he'd made it to the porch. "John. Oh, John, it's so good to see you again."

"Hello, Minnie, how have you been? I sure was sorry to hear about your tragedy with the boys."

"Please come in, I've just made a pot of fresh coffee. There's blueberry jam and fresh bread. I know that's your favorite," Minnie trilled, feeling giddy as a school girl. The couple talked awhile. Minnie was attuned to the tingling sensation that seemed to flow throughout her body in his presence. He was handsome as ever, she thought inwardly; the same chiseled features, the lines of his jaw, piercing blue eyes, clean-cut mannerisms and his subtle aura of manliness.

The timber baron's thoughts drifted across Minnie's tantalizing shapeliness as she sat demurely at the kitchen table. "Are you getting along alright?" he asked, concentrating on her loveliness.

"Yes, I'm doin' fine."

There was an embarrassing silence as his eyes caressed her voluptuous figure. The years have been good to her, he thought. She's as beautiful as ever.

Noticing the rifle hanging on the wall prompted Kennedy to ask her, "Where's Henry?" as he helped himself to a second slice of bread and jam.

"I dunno. He's been gone a long time. Just up and left one day," she said, becoming quite self-conscious under his gaze.

"How are you going to manage with the farm and all?"

"Had a good crop of spuds. Hired a couple of hands to help me with the harvest. Now I've got a tidy sum in the bank. But spring might be a different story," she continued, steepling her roughened

This picture of Giles Quimby was thought to have been taken at the then abandoned Pillashak shortly after the shoot-out at Tornow Lake.

fingers reflectively off her smooth-complexioned chin. "Don't know if I'll plant a crop or just sell this place. He ain't comin' back, I'm almost sure of that. So I can do whatever I want," she told him with a sideways glance to determine if he noticed her nervousness.

In the east, the early-dawn sky continued to drowse in starlight as the first awakening winter robins and black-capped chickadees twittered their welcoming songs to the coming new day. John and Minnie had chatted and visited the night away but now it was time to leave before the winter's morning sun broke across the horizon. Kennedy mused how pleasant the evening had passed in Minnie's company. He climbed into the mud-splattered Reo and slowly drove up the slickened road. He felt on top of the world, only one thing bothered him. Got to get this filthy car washed, he thought to himself. Can't stand dirty things.

* * *

Edward Tornow was now the sole occupant of the home place that his industrious parents, Fritz and Louisa, had settled and developed into a self-sufficient farm. The other three boys; William, Albert and Frederick, now grown men in their thirties, had scattered to various jobs and Pacific Northwest logging camps.

Following the murders of the Bauer twins, Edward seldom saw his sister, Minnie Bauer, even though they each lived alone and only a couple of miles from each other. Henry had mysteriously disappeared. Lizzy, the only surviving Bauer youngster lived in town, and Edward had outlasted the Tornow clan on the family homestead. The feuding, innuendos and suspicions———especially the unproven suspicions—had taken their toll on brother and sister down through the years.

Minnie was quoted in newspaper stories at the time as believing her brother John was innocent of killing her twins. "I ain't sayin' who I think killed the boys, but I know in my heart it wasn't John." Although she seldom, if ever, saw her fugitive baby brother, Minnie continued to express her sisterly love and admiration for him. Perhaps her role in nursing him through the black measles and near-fatal fever had forged a durable bond of affection so dedicated as to withstand the most severe test of suspicion and accusation.

As the Pacific Northwest winter storms began to diminish early in 1912, land developer J.B. Lucas paid Edward Tornow a visit. There had been charges and counterclaims levelled by upper-Satsop valley land owners regarding county timber assessments, ownership, log rustling and decreased forestland revenues. Lucas was familiar with these problems and he knew how to successfully litigate them.

Driving up the narrow road Lucas mused how Edward fit into the intricate financial puzzle that was evolving within the fledgling timber industry. There was also the estate of the Tornow elders and implications concerning Edward and John Tornow. Many issues remained unresolved.

* * *

Colorful blossoms and fresh, new growth burst upon the countryside in early spring of 1912. At higher elevations, avalanche lilies and perky western trilliums seemed to race melting snowbanks for a place in the vibrant sunshine. The forest vegetation literally exploded as tender new buds popped out almost overnight from the warming trend. Chattering and frolicking with renewed energy, the birds and small animals returned to their familiar haunts.

John Tornow also emerged from his self-imposed winter dormancy. Standing straight and upright in the subdued spring sunshine, he stretched tall from his toes to the tips of his wilderness-stained fingers. He watched, listened, and gathered up the sounds, sights and smells of his cherished mountain retreat. His thoughts next turned to food, his winter supply was almost depleted. Gone was Mother Nature's bountiful larder of smoked venison, fruits, nuts, berries, and edible roots and bulbs he had harvested before winter arrived.

Bands of elk were returning to the foothills. As a shopper would prepare to go to the market, John grabbed his rifle and began looking for a young cow elk or deer that would provide him with fresh meat.

In complete silence, the hunter ghosted through the stands of Douglas firs in search of game. Out of nowhere, a darkish-brown whirr of wings startled him as a spruce grouse took frightened flight from beneath his feet. John chuckled, "One of you chickens surely would taste good roasted over an open fire." He made a mental note to try his hand at catching grouse since they had returned from the lowlands.

Half-hidden through the alders, he saw an open hillside nature had wrought from a lightning caused forest fire. New growth had already begun rejuvenating the fire-scarred slope with a stand of young mountain alder which marched up the steep hill in random profiles. Elk often fed on low-growing berry and sorrel brush growing in those open areas; small shrubs nourished by the sunshine, rich in nutrients that would replenish fat and body tone diminished during winter.

John stopped in the edge of timber, surveying the hillside for game. His eyes filled with desire as he saw a large bull standing guard over a band of ten or twelve cows and yearlings. John knew it was a bull even though the animal had no antlers. As they did every year, the massive elk had shed his rack and would grow a new set during the spring and summer. He would hone them to fighting fitness in time for the challenge of other amorous bulls during the fall rutting season.

John had no desire to shoot the old bull; too big, too tough and too lean after he'd fought off horny competitors all season. But a yearling cow who appeared to have wintered well caught the hunter's attention. That one will make good camp meat, he thought to himself.

The cow had just risen from her daytime bed. A natural act upon awakening, she stretched her muscles and invigorated her body, preparing to feed on tender willow shoots growing in a low swale on the hillside. With caution born of instinct she first took time to find out what was happening around her. She watched, she listened, and she

154

raised her muzzle to test the wind for any smell of danger.

Suddenly her ears stood straight up, pointed at John like two antennae tuned to gather the slightest sound. She stiffened, staring straight at him; something was different over there; she sensed it was different from the last time she'd looked.

John knew he was being thoroughly scrutinized by the animal. He froze, staring back. His every instinct was synchronized to precision sharpness, matching wilderness aptitudes with this creature of the mountains. It was a competitive game of intuitive senses, although the animal was far superior in smelling and hearing.

Still as a monolith, frozen in place, he could hear the low bleatings of the nearby elk calves; smell the animals' musky odor as it blended with the dank marshy aroma of the wet hillside bog where they fed.

From inexperience, coupled with hunger, the young cow decided her surroundings were safe. She dropped her gaze at John to nibble tender twigs.

A fatal decision. Like a predator awaiting a split-second opportunity, John instantly threw the rifle to his shoulder as the elk's attention was diverted. The single killing shot dropped the animal where she stood. He hoped nobody was near the hillside to hear the rifle's bark, to detect his presence.

John sliced the venison in long strips that would be easy to hang on green alder poles for curing. He was more than a mile from his closest concealed camp. Making two trips, he managed to carry all the meat he needed.

Relaxing that evening around his small campfire of seasoned fir and red cedar, John felt good after his first meal of fresh meat in several weeks. He built larger meat-curing fires at night when the smoke couldn't be detected. Orange flames danced high above the quick burning dry wood as pitch pockets ignited, making a firecracker popping noise.

He often spent time trying to figure out what had happened to make people come after him all the time. "I ain't done nothin'," he muttered, throwing another dry stick on the fire. "I'm just an ordinary man." But the bothersome inner voice disagreed with him. He heard it echoing in his ears, *Maybe you did somethin' you've forgot about. But be careful, they're out to get you. Be real careful, John, don't let 'em catch you.*

He heard it warning him time after time, he couldn't shut the voice out of his mind. He stood up, ran behind a big spruce tree trying to get away from it. The voice was still there. He clambered on top an immense blow-down cedar, still there. As a last resort, John went into his shack of limbs and bark slabs, laid down on his bed of dry moss. Out of desperation he clapped his hands over his ears to smother the troublesome inner voice. It wouldn't go away.

With modern sophistication that was not available in 1912, significant psychological evaluation into John's personality profile would have undoubtedly revealed tendencies towards schizophrenia. His loss of contact with society, and disorder of feeling, thought and conduct would have suggested a potential affliction. Perhaps the severe fever in early childhood was contributory. Some researchers believe John was born missing a normal need for social interaction. These shortcomings, however, would not have made him a vicious killer. Instead, the persecution and harassment by inconsiderate officials and relatives seemed to be a primary influence that forced him into his role as a solitary forest loner.

* * *

Not everyone welcomed the advent of warmer spring weather. For trappers Louis Blair and Frank Getty their productive season was almost over for the year. "Have you noticed the fur is beginning to lose it's prime?" Getty asked his partner one day in late February as they inspected their week's catch at their primitive camp in the Olympic foothills.

"Yeah, guess we'd best pull our traps and head out," Blair replied. "This early spring is gonna hit us in the pocketbook."

Getty nodded. "It sure will. It'll hit us hard."

As the two men began hiking out of the forest wilderness, they came upon the remains of the cow elk John Tornow had shot just a week earlier.

"Poachers," Getty said. "You ever see the work of poachers before? Real wasteful."

"I'm not so sure about that," Blair replied. "Look at how the meat was removed. A poacher would take it by quarters, probably bone it out to reduce the weight. Whoever did this cut the meat off in long strips."

"Yeah, you're right," Getty said. "I once saw some Indians strip meat that way. They hung the strips to dry and then made it into jerky."

The possible answer hit both men at almost the same instant. "Are you thinkin' the same thing I am?" Blair asked as he stared in speculation at his partner.

"John Tornow," Getty said, now speaking in a soft voice like he was afraid John might be listening.

"Certainly is possible. He's been known to hang around this part of the Oxbow country."

"Soon as we get back to Montesano we'd best report this to the sheriff," Getty exclaimed, hurrying his arms into the shoulder straps of his bulky packsack.

"Yes, report it as soon as possible," Blair echoed.

The trappers were vigilant in the extreme as they cautiously hiked down from the Olympic foothills. Coming face-to-face with the fugitive on the trail was not something they wanted to do even though both had met and talked with John in past years. His reputation as

157

the supposed, "Wild Man of the Oxbow" made many people reluctant to enter the forest. Even the back streets of a few Olympic Peninsula settlements, streets that extended a short distance into the wilderness, were being avoided by some overcautious residents. Mothers used the Tornow legend to frighten obedience from their children, telling them, "You'd better behave or John Tornow will get you." An overzealous public, in particular the urban dwellers, through unfounded fear, accusation, and hearsay was methodically imprinting the outlaw title onto John Tornow's name.

* * *

When the trappers reported finding the elk carcass, Sheriff Payette pursed his lips like he'd sucked a lemon. "Hmmm, very interesting," he mused. "I wonder. Could it have been done by John Tornow? If it was him I'm a bit surprised he made it through the winter. We ain't heard nothing about him since last fall," the sheriff said, steepling his fingers like a tent.

"Well, we didn't hang around to find out if John had killed the elk," Getty said. "All we wanted was out of there," he emphasized with a quick swish of his arm over his head.

"Yeah, out of there in a hurry," Blair reiterated, his eyes narrowing as he spoke.

Sheriff Payette called for a confab with a couple of his deputies to determine how to follow-up on this latest report. "This sounds like a good lead," he said, leaning back on just two legs of his wooden chair and staring at the ceiling like he expected the answer to be written there in big letters. "John would be hungry for meat after the long winter, taking venison strips would make sense because he'd be smoking it that way," Payette concluded.

Deputy Colin McKenzie, part-time Aberdeen photographer, clasped his hands behind his head and stared in deep thought out the window at the early spring rains pelting the narrow gravel street around the courthouse. "Maybe we should follow-up on this just to find out who's been killing elk out of season," he suggested.

"I don't think we should go chasing up the Satsop with a big hootin' and hollerin' posse," Payette said. "If this should be Tornow's work, we'd just spook him out of there," he said, dropping the chair back down on all four legs with a resounding thump. "What do you think of that, Colin?"

"I agree, besides if you send me up there I think I could talk John into surrendering without a fight."

"If there's an opportunity, by all means any good lawman should consider talking before using force," the sheriff said. "But I think relying just on words to bring John in would be a mistake. A fatal mistake. You might find yourself looking at daisies from the wrong end," he said, smiling as he lightly brushed his fingers across the badge pinned to his khaki shirt.

"Can I go check it out, sheriff?" McKenzie asked. He was a native of Canada, of slight build, a diligent tracker and a rugged outdoorsman. McKenzie had participated in the hunt for Tornow the previous fall after he'd led the posse that discovered the bodies of the Bauer twins. The deputy had made no secret of his opinion that the search for Tornow should not have been curtailed in November. Now he was eager to once again hit the trail of the woods loner.

"Why don't we ask that game warden, Al Elmer, to go with you?" Payette suggested.

"That's all right with me, he sure knows that country. Matter of fact I think he's in the courthouse right now. I saw him in the hall awhile ago."

Later, giving the two men their instructions, the sheriff said, "I want you boys to go find that elk carcass. Be careful and look around to determine if Tornow is in that part of the country." Wagging his index finger to press home his point, he directed them, "Under no circumstances do I want you going after Tornow. Just scout the area and report back to me. If it looks promising, we'll take a big posse up there to apprehend him. Blair and Getty can draw you a map to the elk carcass. Any questions?"

A.V. Elmer had been a Pacific Northwest game warden for more than a dozen years and knew the country between the Satsop and Wynooche rivers from many first-hand experiences. A lightweight, like McKenzie, he was lean and wiry, could hike mountains for days without stopping. Both had a love for the outdoors. "Colin tells me he thinks he could talk John Tornow into coming in peacefully, but I disagree with him. I think it will require force, maybe worse," Elmer told Payette.

"I don't want either of you getting close enough to him to find out," the sheriff said. "Consider him armed and very dangerous."

Payette deputized Elmer the next day and the two men then gathered up provisions for a week's stay in the woods. They obtained a map from Blair and Getty to locate the elk carcass. The deputies drove one of the county's Ford patrol cars to road's end, about twenty-five miles into the Olympic foothills.

"Well, now the fun begins," McKenzie said, parking the Model-T off the side of the road. He grabbed his full packsack, .30 calibre rifle, and strapped on his sidearm, a German-made Luger pistol.

"Yep, we'll be on our foot-bones from here," Elmer acknowledged, slamming the Ford's door. With a casual hop he stepped off the black steel running board, shouldering his .25-.20 carbine.

"We've got all afternoon and the weather's looking tolerable," McKenzie said. "Do you suppose we can find that old trapper's cabin that Blair and Getty described? We could stay there tonight then strike out on the trail at first light in the morning."

"Sure thing. I know where it is. Fritz Dunkelburger built it about ten years ago. I once caught a fellow there who had been

160

poaching deer out of season. He was guilty as sin, judge sent him up for thirty days."

And so these two lawmen began their hike into the virginal wilderness through the magnificent stands of sharp-needled, Sitka spruce and western hemlock, toward the snow-capped mountains of

The body of John Tornow, killed on April 16, 1913, after eluding lawmen in the wilds of Western Washington State for nineteen months.

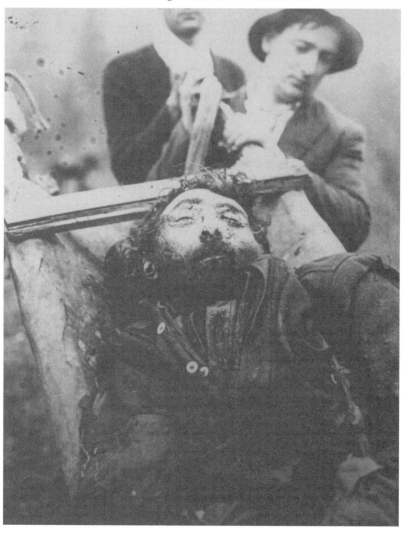

blue-gray basalt rock the color of ancient stone fortresses, past the swift-flowing turbid river far below in the deep, green canyon. They set forth into eternity.

Trudging upwards to the foothills, McKenzie and Elmer peered down to marshy ravines where the unmistakable, brilliant yellow hues of early emerging skunk cabbage plants contrasted with dark, soggy swamplands. The soil was black, steaming with richness, smelling of spring. Canyons were guarded with formidable spears of spiny devil's club, Mother Nature's own thorny barrier deceptively adorned with enticing red berries.

The timberland they passed through was a five or six mile- wide corridor flanked between the Wynooche and Satsop rivers, both of which had their origin in the Olympics; they were born out of melting snows and torrents of rainforest precipitation. It was a magnificent country.

Although both deputies were outdoors-smart and fugitive-wary, the trek to the trapper's cabin that March day of 1912 was not without apprehension. They knew Tornow could be anywhere; behind rocks or trees, perhaps in the evergreen limbs above them, maybe waiting in a brushy ambush beside the trail. "Keep a sharp lookout," McKenzie warned, holding his rifle in readiness across his chest.

The deputies were uncertain about Tornow's reaction should they meet him. Would he shoot, or would he befriend them? These serious questions romped through their minds but there were no answers!

The game warden worried as he checked his carbine once again to make sure a cartridge was in the firing chamber. He was concerned about this hike through Tornow country. Elmer thought to himself, What am I doing here? I'm a game protector, not a lawman. I'm not paid to risk my life with wild fugitives. But I'd agreed to go, can't back out now.

Although not working partners they were now united—two wary officers, not in reality frightened, but both were apprehensive.

162

Romantic music danced through Minnie's head on that spring morning as she busied herself tidying up the cabin and planning the midday meal for company. Shimmering heat rays rose from the huge blackened cookstove as she piled in the wood to maintain a constant oven baking temperature. The aroma in the warm farmhouse promised savory delights in the making.

Her wasp-waisted figure and creamy-smooth skin belied her forty-five years. The nimble bounce in her step served to affirm the ageless influence created by her new carefree lifestyle. She'd squandered five dollars for the attractive dress she'd long admired on the rack behind the men's shoe department at the General Store. Oh, no! She wouldn't put it on yet, John Kennedy wasn't coming for dinner 'til twelve. Mustn't risk getting spots on the sparkling blue gingham.

She glanced at the gold watch hanging by a thong from the cabin's log wall. Only eleven, she noted, got plenty of time before he gets here.

When the temperature was just right she popped a rich, double-crust blueberry pie, his favorite, into the oven. Minnie had killed one of Henry's beloved chickens and it was stewing in the big blue-enamel pot on the back of the stove. Thinking how he used to pamper and protect those cackling leghorns, she smiled a satisfied little smile as she lifted the lid and poked the hen's carcass with a sharp fork. She was content with the thought that Henry was out of her life for good. He was gone and she was better off for it.

With dinner prepared, Minnie slipped into her new store-bought dress. She paused a moment to reflect, this was her first, her very first new dress. All the others had been hand-me-downs or homemade. She felt elegant as a queen, getting gussied up for the grand ball. Minnie couldn't resist the temptation to pirouette around the bed; her bed where she'd spent so much time pretending, never dreaming there could be such a richer, fuller life as she was experiencing. She swished the long dress, acting out her euphoria of contentment.

Minnie heard the automobile when it was still on top the hill, a mile or so up the road from the cabin. He was coming, almost here. She could not quite contain herself. She rushed to the door, then stopped lightning-quick. Mustn't appear too eager, she thought. Wait 'til he knocks.

She risked a peek out the tiny window as the Reo pulled into the yard and stopped with an emphatic bang as Kennedy shut down the engine. She stood just inside the door, smoothed her dress one last time, patted her hair gently making sure all tresses were in place.

Kennedy's knock and her opening the door were almost simultaneous, surprising the timber tycoon. "Good morning, Minnie, I'm glad you were expecting me." He stopped and handed her a green paper-wrapped bouquet of red roses as he entered the house.

"For me?" she exclaimed. "Flowers for me? Oh, John, they're beautiful."

"I'd hoped you'd like them. Had them sent in special delivery on the train yesterday. Can't get nice things like these in Matlock, at least not this time of year."

Minnie carefully placed the flowers on the table, dropped into a chair—in fact it had been Henry's favorite chair—and buried her head in her hands, weeping in tiny sobs.

Dressed in his natty gabardine suit like he'd just stepped off the pages of Esquire magazine, John stooped in front of Minnie. A troubled look crossed his handsome face as he asked, "What's wrong? Why are you crying?"

She shook her head, hiding her face with both hands so he couldn't see her tears. "Nothin', ain't nothin' wrong, I'm just so happy, just so very happy, John."

"I don't understand. If you're happy, why the tears?"

"You might not savvy this but when I seen the flowers it made me think. Would you believe? I even hate to admit it—that's the first time a man has ever brought me flowers. The very first time. I love you for doing it," she smiled at him through her tear-streaked face. On the huge, blackened cookstove, the stewing hen—Henry's prized leghorn—continued to simmer cheerful bubbles and send a tantalizing aroma throughout the country home.

✳ ✳ ✳

McKenzie and Elmer arrived at the rough-hewn trapper's shack by mid-afternoon. It was small, about the size of a one-car garage. It had a split-shake, steep-pitched roof so heavy winter snows wouldn't stick.

"There she be," Elmer said, "just as I remembered it. Hope the skunks ain't messed up the insides."

"It'll do for tonight," McKenzie said, "we might need a roof over our heads before morning. There's a feel of rain in the air."

The crude cabin didn't have a stove or fireplace so the two deputies prepared supper over an outside campfire built where others had done the same. Following their sparse meal, the men pored over the map drawn by Blair and Getty. They studied it like tourists planning the next day's excursion. "From what the trappers said I'd put the elk carcass maybe two or three miles from here. We should get there by mid-morning," McKenzie said.

They awoke early—very early—to a light mist that was sifting down through the forest canopy as they stepped outside. After a swig of stiff coffee bubbled over a quick campfire, they were on their way through a heavy stand of old-growth Douglas firs. They soon found a well-used elk trail that meandered up the ridge, but later became more difficult to follow in the gray, early morning drizzle.

"We're gettin' closer and closer to Tornow country," McKenzie said, "it's time to stay wide awake."

The muddy old path zigzagged between stately firs where an understory of dark green sword ferns and brushy huckleberry foliage softened the rock-strewn mountainous terrain. Taller than a man's head in places the jungle-like growth could provide numerous ambush points along the trail. Recognizing this lethal potential, both deputies kept nervous fingers on their triggers. After a couple of hours McKenzie looked out of the dark timber and saw the open hillside ahead. He whispered to his partner, "Al, that looks like the opening marked on the map. I'll bet the elk carcass is right out there in the middle."

"I think I can see the blazed tree the trappers said they marked. Let's take a look, Colin."

They leaned their rifles against a half-burnt, blow-down tree from the lightning fire. After nearly two weeks, the carcass was getting quite ripe and had been visited by several forest scavengers. Holding his nose, McKenzie said, "Not much we can learn here, let's see if we can pick up a trail he might have used leaving the carcass."

Searching the ground for man tracks, Elmer soon called McKenzie over to a spot of bare dirt that had been scuffed. "Yep, that's the direction he went when he left." Stooping close to the track, he pointed at the indention, "Look how deep he sank into the dirt, must have been carrying something heavy, like elk meat."

"That old animal trail he's on is heading for the top of the ridge," Elmer said. "That's going farther into the mountains. If it was a poacher, he'd be heading downhill towards civilization with the meat. Those tracks were made by a big man, chances are we're looking at the footprints of John Tornow would be my guess." "The sheriff said to be careful but let's follow this trail a ways and see if we can eliminate any doubt we're on Tornow's tracks," McKenzie said.

"All right, you lead the way," Elmer suggested. "I've heard you've got a nose like a bloodhound for this sort of thing."

Smiling, McKenzie replied, "Well, yeah, I've done it a few times. Caught a few who didn't think they could be caught."

The fine gray mist continued to float in a lazy veil over the terrain, inundating the entire countryside, throwing a soggy wet blanket over everything. A pair of Mallard ducks skimmed low over the tree-tops, gaggeling their approval of the wet weather.

At trail's edge, a winter-denuded black gooseberry bush was host to an intrepid wolf spider who had bridged a span between two dark-brown limbs. The intricate patterned, dew-covered web swayed gracefully in the gentle mountain breeze.

* * *

He cussed the damp drizzle. He could get along right well without this, he thought, moving the hanging strips of venison into the lean-to out of the rain from where they'd been air curing.

Suddenly he stopped and listened. He'd heard the branch snap, not just any old snap but a branch breaking sound made by a man's heavy foot, unlike any animal noise. John Tornow slowly reached for his rifle and peered out from the blow-down trees where he'd built his clever hideout. His dark eyes shone with malice, he could hear somebody approaching. Must be somebody who'd found the elk carcass. And now they were coming after him.

Chapter Seven

A GRAY JAY, LOOKING MUCH LIKE A HUGE, OVERGROWN CHICKADEE, peered with uncertainty into the well-hidden camp. The bird was hungry for a scrap of meat it had spotted hanging on poles, but not brave enough to risk the ire of the bushy-haired man holding the rifle. A slight breeze intensified the morning's damp drizzle. It rocked the bird's perch atop the slender, noble fir bristling with bluish-green needles and diamond-like rain droplets.

There! He heard another limb snap. Not a loud noise but enough to draw John Tornow's attention. Somewhere a squirrel chirruped raucously, interrupting John's concentration on the closer sound. The furry wilderness tattletale was scolding something; a predator, another squirrel, perhaps a man intruder. The forest always echoes a recurrent resonance, sometimes quiet, other times noisy.

"Wish that damned squirrel would shut up," McKenzie whispered to Elmer, moving in close 'til he was nearly speaking into his ear, hunched up in his slicker against the morning drizzle.

"Yeah, the little varmint could alert somebody that we're here," Elmer turned, whispering back. "The tracks of this guy carrying the venison are still following this trail."

In apprehension, both deputies continued to scan the surrounding countryside, trying to pick up any movement indicating they were not alone. Tension crackled in the air.

John Tornow quietly moved over to the farthest blow-down tree and sat beside it, resting is chin on the top log. He had cunningly built his camp in a triangular area formed by several downed firs. Like the walls of a fortress, his shelter was surrounded by the waist-high logs. Winter winds had toppled the trees, forming a natural, double-walled barricade.

John's dark eyes narrowed, straining to catch sight of any intruder approaching his forest sanctuary. Now a hush descended, cloaking the woods in silence. He gripped his Winchester with dirty hands that hadn't seen soap in months. The loner's anxiety intensified as his haunting inner-voice warned him, *Careful John, somebody's comin'.*

Twenty feet away an enormous red cedar tree, eight feet in diameter, had blown down, blocking the trail. There was a two foot opening beneath the giant log. A man could continue on the path, but entrance required crawling under the tree on hands and knees like a child at play. From behind his fortress-like camp John now stared intently at the opening. Anyone tracking him would have to crawl under that cedar log.

Like a well-trained field general, the fugitive had carefully selected his sanctuary; choosing the lay of the land should he be forced to defend himself from intruders bent on disrupting his solitary existence.

Not suspecting they had only three hundred yards to live, McKenzie and Elmer sat on a log to rest and discuss their strategy. The pair sat beside each other so their low whispers wouldn't carry through the air. Off the lower end of the ridge a patch of blue sky appeared above the dull-gray overcast. A brilliant hued, double rainbow glistened through the hazy mist over the conifer forested valley. But nature's brilliance could not overcome the ominous scene that was unfolding.

Elmer's low, raspy voice betrayed his anxiety, "Seems to me it's almost a sure bet we're on Tornow's trail. Why don't we go back and tell the sheriff so he can send in a posse?"

169

Thoughtfully stroking his stubbled chin like it would help him think, McKenzie whispered, "I'd like to get a bit more proof. We might be following some sod buster who just poached that elk to feed his family."

Resigned to his disappointment about not soon heading back, Elmer's answer was sharp as a whiplash, "A sod buster sure as hell wouldn't be going in this direction."

John sat motionless behind his log barricade. The woods creature's ears were attuned to pick up and sift through all the wilderness sounds on that drizzly March morning. He was patient as a cat waiting out a mouse.

They're out there, I know they are, he thought to himself. In a moment he heard another sound. It was the troublesome inner-voice. *They're comin' after you, better look out. You'll be sorry if you let 'em catch you. Remember what your brother did to Cougar? Remember how Uncle Henry tongue-lashed Sis? You gotta stop 'em, John.*

Listening to the tiny voice, John's wild, dark eyes rolled furtively across the scene in front of him. He was almost out of control, somewhat resembling the fabled madman description that had been pinned on him. A cartridge was in his Winchester's firing chamber. It was loaded with 170 grains of lead just waiting to inflict death and destruction upon its victim.

Half-hidden through the green fir branches, Elmer spotted the gray jay perched in the top of the slender young noble fir tree. It made him wonder. Jays, commonly called camp robbers at logging camps, usually hang out around people where they beg for table scraps. He thought, are we getting close to someone's camp? Maybe John Tornow's camp?

"We can't go around, guess we'll have to crawl under this blowdown cedar," McKenzie said in a soft voice.

"Yeah, crawl under, I'll go first," Elmer repeated. He took off his

Posse poses with John Tornow's body at abandoned Pillashak homestead. Members are unidentified but tall man with suspenders was thought to be Sheriff Mathews.

packsack, got down on all fours and pushed the pack ahead of him. Elmer held his carbine in one hand as he crawled, hands before knees, through the narrow opening.

"I'm right behind you so keep moving," McKenzie whispered.

The inner-voice suddenly shouted in John Tornow's ears, *There's one of 'em, get him!*

John threw his U.S. .30 calibre rifle to his shoulder, ready to shoot. Then recognized it was a packsack being slid beneath the log. What's this? It wasn't a man. He paused, holding up his rifle. In just a matter of seconds John next saw the man's head, bigger than life, appear in the narrow opening. The hammer was cocked; he was ready to protect his loner existence. He needed only to pull the trigger.

Tiny droplets from the morning's drizzle clung to the smooth rifle barrel, hanging there like a drippy faucet.

Elmer thought to himself as he crawled through the opening, damn, we're helpless as fish in a barrel while in this position on our hands and knees. But he had to keep crawling, McKenzie was right behind, bumping him to hurry. Soon as he had cleared the huge obstacle, the game warden lost no time getting onto his feet.

His weight hadn't yet transferred to his legs. All of a sudden the wilderness silence was torn by an earsplitting rifle blast. Elmer never heard it. The bullet that splattered his chest and ripped his heart to a mass of pulpy tissue had travelled faster than the sound of the shot. Now limp and lifeless his body crumpled to the ground. Blood gushed from the gaping hole in his chest and stained the damp forest floor with a huge red splotch.

John's inner-voice was jubilant. *That's the way, you got him, that was good shootin'.*

It had been almost point-blank range. Just a few feet away. As John had always done since his Pa taught him, he just threw the gun up, looked down the sightless rifle barrel and shot by instinct. He was accurate. Murderously accurate.

McKenzie, still on his hands and knees, had heard the rifle blast. As Elmer's rag-doll body slumped to the ground, it just missed falling on top of him. In his anxiety, the deputy struggled to locate the source of the shot. He hobbled sideways to avoid Elmer's lifeless body, trying in desperation to regain his balance and get into position to return the fire.

McKenzie raised his upper body, standing low on his knees in the soft wet ground. The deputy frantically looked behind the log barricade for the killer. In a split second he saw the fugitive's shaggy head peering at him over the top of a fallen tree.

Right after the first shot, John had worked his rifle's lever action, ejecting the hot, spent cartridge casing and replacing it with a live round. Then he became aware of his dwindling ammunition supply, maybe only one or two left, he thought to himself.

He saw McKenzie's upper body appear at the same precise instant McKenzie spotted him behind the log. John's instinctive shooting without taking time to sight gave him a fractional advantage.

The forest loner beat McKenzie to the draw by only a milli-second, but it was enough. The deputy had seen John behind the log and was in the act of drawing down on him when Tornow's white-hot bullet ripped into his shoulder, tearing the rifle from his grasp. McKenzie writhed on the ground. He screamed with pain, his shoulder and upper left chest a bloody mess of torn flesh and shattered bone fragments.

In an instant, the devilish inner-voice sounded in John's ear. *He ain't dead and you're near out of bullets, better do somethin' John, and do it fast. If you don't, he's just as liable as not to shoot you like Edward shot your dog.*

The deputy now lay shrieking on the ground. John almost went berserk from the haunting voice and frightening turn of events. He noted for the first time that McKenzie was wearing a sidearm. *Get it! Get it and kill him with his own gun,* John heard. Jumping out from behind the log he raced to McKenzie's writhing body and snatched the Luger from it's holster.

The deputy looked up helplessly at his wild-eyed tormentor knowing what was happening but unable to do anything about it. Deep shock from his wound had now paralyzed him; but his thought process continued to function, alerting him to John's actions. He knew he was going to die. Unable to defend himself, McKenzie realized death was inevitable.

Clutching the pistol, John leaped on top the log closest to McKenzie's bloody, still-pulsating body. Staring up at his scraggy executioner the still-conscious deputy was the first to witness the terribly contorted, maniacal sneer; the hateful, deadly gaze in John's dark eyes, the threatening low growl from deep in his throat, the sinister appearance of a now crazed murderer.

For a brief moment McKenzie looked into the black, deadly hole that was the barrel-end of his own Luger. The pistol shots echoed twice in the stillness of the remote Olympic foothills. And then the deputy's suffering ended. It ended with two merciful bullets. McKenzie's pain had ceased but John Tornow's was only beginning.

The scene was quiet as a graveyard; quiet as death scenes always are when the killing has ended. A cloud of heavy blue-gray smoke from the shooting hung in the cool, misty air. The smell of gunpowder, mingled with the horrible stench of death, overpowered the usual pleasant forest fragrance.

Frightened by the shots, the gray jay had considered taking flight to quieter places. But its hunger for a taste of the hanging venison had kept the skittish bird perched on the young noble fir tree. Now there were three men but two appeared asleep. Maybe there's still a chance I might have a reach at that meat, the bird mused.

John sat on a log staring at the bodies. As if mesmerized, he swayed back and forth, emitting a low, throaty wail like a father who had just lost a son. The troublesome inner-voice that goaded him to madness was satiated. The maniacal influence that had transformed him into a killer was still. Now, reality had set in. And reality told him he'd done wrong. His mother's voice reading, "Thou shalt not kill," echoed through the stillness and a tear of remorse rolled down his grizzled cheek.

He slipped a grimy hand under McKenzie's head to make certain the deputy was dead. In an instant he pulled back, repulsed by fingers covered with warm, thick blood oozing from McKenzie's head wound. So much blood. A crimson pool filled the forest floor beneath the bodies. Almost nauseated, John wiped his hand in the damp grass. But he couldn't wipe away the terrible feelings trapped within his conscience.

John kept a quiet vigil at the carnage until late afternoon. The drizzle had stopped but the cooler air shocked him back to reality. First, he removed the outer clothing from the bodies, leaving them clothed in their long underwear. He'd been wearing the same ragged clothing for close to six months. Although both men were much smaller than John, he improvised and discarded his tattered garments.

Noticing McKenzie was wearing almost new caulked (hobnail) boots, the fugitive slipped them off. But he realized they were several sizes too small for him. A couple of slashes with his sheath knife allowed his bigger feet to slide tightly into the new boots. He left his old ragged shoes and clothes, left them with the bodies, worn-out and discarded.

John welcomed the deputies' weapons and ammunition; his own supply was getting quite low. Searching through their packsacks he began ravenously devouring several hardtack biscuits, his first in many months.

Having decided to bury the bodies, he scratched shallow graves on a nearby hillside out of the soft earth. The haunting inner-voice returned while he was digging. He tried to ignore it but now it seemed to insinuate itself into his every thought and action. *Why not bury 'em like your initial? In the shape of a "T". It'll be "T" for Tornow. Go ahead, do it. Then get the hell out of here. They'll soon be after you again.*

* * *

Spears of bright sunlight beamed through the parlor window as Minnie heard the clatter of a horse and buggy in the rutted dirt yard.

Leaving the hearty beef stew she was fixing, she peered outside to see who was coming. Couldn't be John Kennedy she thought, he always arrives with a bang.

Then she recognized her brother Edward whom she hadn't seen in quite a spell. Wonder what he wants?

She met him on the porch, "Ain't seen you of late. What brings you around, Edward?"

"Hi, Sis, it's been awhile. I thought it was high-time I came over to visit my only sister."

"Coffee's on, come in if you've a mind to," Minnie said flippantly, swishing into the house.

Sitting at the table with a steaming mug of coffee, Edward leaned back in his chair, pushed his hat high on his head and hooked both thumbs through his wide farmer suspenders. Minnie pulled out a chair and eyed him with suspicion across the table. She knew he was up to something.

"I've heard Henry ain't around no more, Sis. Where'd he go?"

"He's gone away, gone for good."

"How you fixin' to run the ranch, you bein' a woman all alone?"

"I'll manage."

"I been thinkin', maybe if you can't handle this place, you might want to sell it to me. Of course I ain't got much money so I couldn't pay much but you'd least-ways get enough to make a new start someplace."

"I ain't decided yet what I'm gonna do," she replied.

Edward continued, "With John being a fugitive and all, he's liable not to come back. I'll more n' likely get his 160 acres that adjoins the home place. Then if I had this quarter-section I could farm 'em all together."

Minnie flushed at this mention of her Baby Brother. "John's gonna come back. He ain't guilty of nothin'."

He calculated his sister over the rim of his mug as he slurped a mouthful of coffee, and whined, "This old place ain't worth much, I'd have to cut the timber and clear most of the land before I could farm it. But if you're gonna have to sell it for a song, might as well sell to your kin."

For many years Minnie had felt uncomfortable around her young brother. The suspicions, the innuendos, her daughter's death, the selfish actions had all taken their toll of his credibility in Minnie's mind. She couldn't push aside the doubts that existed. "I think I'll just hang onto the old place," she said, her eyes now dropping to her coffee mug with finality.

Taken aback, Edward was quick to down the two last gulps of coffee. He stood up ready to leave. "I'm sorry to hear you say that, Sis, but if you should change your mind you know where I'll be."

Minnie watched him cluck-cluck the horse-drawn buggy out of the yard and up the hill. Good riddance, she thought, feeling comfortable with her decision not to sell.

* * *

Six days had passed since Sheriff Payette had dispatched McKenzie and Elmer into the Oxbow country. He'd heard nothing of them, or from them; like they'd just disappeared into a black hole. Finally, on March 18th, a week after the two deputies had entered the woods, the sheriff formed a search posse. They left Montesano by automobile for the wilderness to search for McKenzie and Elmer. The posse was led by Deputy A.L. Fitzgerald, joined by trapper Louis Blair, one of the men who originally found the elk carcass, and Deputy Charles Lathrop. Several others volunteered to join the search.

Arriving at road's end, the posse members shouldered packsacks and rifles for the wilderness search. Deputy Fitzgerald, a dour expression clouding his face, told the others, "I have a spooky feeling about this hunt for them fellows. They've been gone a week and I'm really afraid they've met with foul play,.

Louis Blair answered as the men started up the trail into the foothills, "I agree with you but how about us? Whatever happened to them could happen to us too, you know."

Charley Lathrop was bringing up the rear and carefully checked the group's backtrail to make certain nobody sneaked up on them from behind. "Best we can do is take it slow and easy; make sure we don't walk into an ambush. I'll mind our backside," Blair said, nervously watching more behind than in front.

"Let's hole up in Fritz Dunkelburger's trapper cabin tonight. We can head out fresh in the morning," Blair suggested.

The posse members awoke to a battleship gray morning, no rain, but dark and gloomy. The kind of weather only seagulls enjoyed. The split-log floor of the cabin had been littered with rubbish and a thick layer of dust from previous occupants. Several bearded deputies had turned gray overnight. Their whiskers had picked up the dusty coating while they slept on the dirty floor.

Deputy Fitzgerald held a brief meeting prior to the posse's departure from the cabin the next morning. "Remember boys, this ain't a manhunt for Tornow. The sheriff told me our only assignment was to find out what happened to McKenzie and Elmer. Keep a sharp lookout just in case."

In the early morning light the posse picked up the tracks of the missing deputies although rain and animal prints almost obliterated them from time to time. "Yep, they went this way to the elk carcass," Blair said. There were several nervous trigger-fingers. In apprehension they watched for any movement along the trail's dense underbrush. High above them the white head of a soaring eagle contrasted against the ominous dark sky as the majestic bird drifted on the thermals building beneath murky thunderheads.

"I sure hope John Tornow's left the country if he's responsible for all this," Lathrop whispered to Fitzgerald. Mournful coyote howls floated through the timber, echoing from the valley as they continued hiking deeper into the wilderness.

Soon the trail broke out to an open hillside. "This is it," Blair said. "Now I remember, the elk carcass is right out there on that slope, behind that stand of mountain alder."

Continuing past the elk kill, the posse again picked up the tracks of McKenzie and Elmer on the well-worn animal path. In about an hour Fitzgerald held up his hand like a traffic cop, bringing the posse to a halt.

Bending close to the ground where another trail crossed theirs, the deputy looked in amazement at what he'd found. "Look here," he said as the men gathered around him. "Careful where you step, don't stomp out none of them tracks."

In the damp mud of the intersecting trail they saw a single set of man tracks wearing caulked boots. The tracks were identical to one of the sets of prints they'd been following. "We're tracking McKenzie and Elmer, I'd recognize Colin's new caulked boots anywhere. I was with him when he bought 'em just a couple of weeks ago. Now all of a sudden we're finding those same boot tracks, but alone, crossing this trail of McKenzie and Elmer.

With a puzzled look, Fitzgerald asked Lathrop, "What do you make of this Charley?"

Studying the prints, Lathrop pointed to the single crossing set. "Look how much deeper these have sunk into the mud. Either this second set is a much bigger man or he's carrying something mighty heavy. Maybe both."

"You know what I think?" Fitzgerald said, looking into the distance at the gray, fog-shrouded mountains like a philosopher searching for a clue in the heavens. "I think somebody else is wearing

Colin's caulked boots. I'll bet a dollar to a doughnut someone has done something terrible to Colin and Al. Them boots are on someone else's feet."

Anxious posse faces looked quizzically at each other, then they peered with apprehension into the nearby jungled trail growth as if they expected to see a dozen John Tornows leap out at them. They were nervous; these men were apprehensive. Small beads of perspiration appeared on several brows—and it wasn't even a warm day. Nervous because they were being threatened by a potentially dangerous fugitive. It could be John Tornow but perhaps it was someone else. Fear of the unknown is the greatest fear of all.

"Let's split up," Fitzgerald suggested in a hushed voice, "Charley, you take a couple of the boys, follow the two sets of tracks. I'll take the rest of the posse and backtrack on these single prints made by Colin's boots."

Followed by two of the volunteers, Lathrop was careful to step back on the main trail. He stooped low to the ground so he wouldn't lose sight of the set of double prints on the soft path. "I have a strange feeling we'll all end up in the same place," the deputy said in a subdued voice.

"Maybe so," Fitzgerald replied. "Just in case we run into trouble, let's agree that a signal for help will be two fast shots fired into the air."

As the group split up and departed, most of the men now had one finger on the hammer of their rifle. They were ready to cock and fire in a heartbeat. Some even walked with hammers already cocked back, a dangerous practice but maybe the split-second saving of time would make the difference between life and death. The thought of meeting up with John Tornow was beginning to get to them—all of them.

Fitzgerald realized they were making painstakingly slow progress; taking a few steps, stopping and looking ahead; then a few more steps, stopping again. That was alright with him. We'll take our time to make sure we ain't walking into no trap, he thought. He shivered. For the first time, he noticed his shirt was drenched from perspiration. Surprised, he glanced at the others. They were sweating too. Guess we're all worked-up about maybe running into this guy, he mused.

Without warning, less than an hour after they'd split up, Fitzgerald saw a movement up ahead through the drooping, yellowish-green Douglas fir branches. Reacting at once he hoarsely whispered, "Get down," to the men behind him, signalling with a flat downward push of his palm. Then he too, out of instinct, dropped to the ground on his belly.

He laid there desperately trying to again catch sight of the movement he'd seen. The deputy laying behind him whispered, "What did you see?" Fitzgerald only raised his arm as a signal to be quiet. He inched his upper body off the soft dirt so he could see better.

"There it is again," he whispered loud enough for the others to hear. Then, "Oh hell, it's only a camp robber."

The deputy grinned with embarrassment as he looked back at the other men, "See the jay up there in that little noble fir?" They nodded and grinned back.

"Wait a minute," Fitzgerald said, now standing up but crouching to see through the dense evergreens. "That jay's standing on a pole and he's pecking at something."

Taking just a few more steps, the deputy all at once realized they had stumbled onto a concealed camp. "Take cover," he hissed like an army squad leader as he jumped behind a Sitka spruce, Winchester held up ready for action. Now his rifle hammer was pulled back. He was ready to fire.

They stood behind cover like statues in the forest for what

181

seemed like hours. Then, Fitzgerald courageously risked exposing himself, sneaking back for a huddle with the deputies.

"There's a camp just ahead hidden between those blow-down firs. Can't tell if anyone's there. The jay was standing on a pole, pecking at something, looked like strips of meat. If it was, you know whose camp this is."

"Wonder where Charley and the others are?" a deputy somberly asked.

"They're maybe coming up the ridge from the other side. I'll wager the two trails we were following both end here. You boys cover me, I'm going to belly-crawl a ways and see if anyone's in the camp," Fitzgerald said.

Hearing voices the gray jay hesitated, then abandoned his smorgasbord of dried venison. It had kept him well-fed since the man left almost a week ago. The camp robber flew away but he'd be back. A stash like that was not easy to give up.

Crawling about thirty feet closer to the triangular camp spot, the deputy got near enough to peer over the first fortress log. Perhaps the most gutsy thing he'd ever done and having considerable second thoughts, Fitzgerald eased his chin across the top of the log wall. He halfway expected to hear the shot that would blow his head off. All was quiet. Looking around inside the natural-made fort, he saw bits and pieces of evidence someone had been there of late. A scrap of torn canvas; dried meat sticking to discarded bones; a blackened circle of dirt from a campfire; a large rock rolled up for a seat; even a pile of tattered, discarded clothes.

Confident the place was deserted, the deputy stood up. He waved his backup force into camp. Then he heard a small twig snap behind him. In a flash he swung his rifle in that direction, ready to shoot. Jumping behind one of the logs for concealment, Fitzgerald looked beneath the huge cedar that blocked the main trail. There was

The sheriff's posse brought out on horseback the remains of John Tornow and two deputies he killed, Louis Blair and Charles Lathrop.

movement there. He aimed at the small opening. Heart pounding, he waited and soon recognized the head of Charley Lathrop poking through the tunnel-like hole.

With a great sigh of relief, Fitzgerald lowered his rifle. He yelled at the arriving deputy, "You're mighty lucky, I nearly blew your head off."

"You're the lucky one, I saw you behind that log, thought you was Tornow, almost ready to shoot when you yelled." Careless fire often causes more casualties than the intentional stuff, Lathrop thought to himself.

On all fours, they crawled under the eight-foot cedar. Standing up, Lathrop pointed to the ground, "That looks like blood—lots of blood—and over there, look, empty cartridge casings scattered on that ground-cover of tangle moss."

Everyone gathered around, Fitzgerald was first to speak. "This don't look good; too much blood, and those empties, pistol shells— McKenzie packed a sidearm, didn't he?"

"He wore a German Luger."

"I'll bet those shells are from his pistol," Fitzgerald solemnly said. "Let's spread out, see what we can find."

In just a few minutes a shout went up, "Over here." With broken stubs of dried limbs the posse soon unearthed the bodies of Deputy Colin McKenzie and deputized game warden, Al Elmer. McKenzie's face was still contorted in a horrible grimace reflecting the last dreadful image he'd had of his tormentor. The shallow graves had been dug in the form of a "T", McKenzie laying crosswise at Elmer's feet. The shocked and silent posse members sat around the death site in paralyzed disbelief. They were unable to comprehend the grisly murders of these two lawmen—neighbors, fellow officers—most had known them as longtime friends in the tight-knit little community. No manly dignity stopped the tears from rolling down the cheeks of these hardened outdoorsmen. Unashamed, they dried their grief-teared eyes on sweat-stained bandanas.

Why? Why were they killed in cold blood? Was it the work of a madman? The deputies were in total agreement when Louis Blair, wiping tears and blowing his nose, with furrowed brow said, "John Tornow must have done this. I suppose something's snapped in his head."

"Have you boys ever seen the work of a madman?" Lathrop asked. "A real maniac? This is what they do."

"It's kind of strange," Fitzgerald said. "Colin had said all along that he thought he could talk Tornow into surrendering without a fight. Now look what his mistake has cost him."

"Well anyway," Blair said, "Al knew what he was talkin' about. From the first get-go he predicted John wouldn't come in peaceful. Guess the game warden knew our fugitive better than us. But he died to prove his point."

"I kind of agree with Colin's thinking," Fitzgerald added. "Not that I'd stake my life on it. But what we're seeing is Tornow's defense of his wanting to be left alone. In his twisted mind, we're all his enemies out to get him. You can't convince me that these killings are natural for the country boy."

"I, for one, never thought he killed his nephews," Blair said. "Maybe we shouldn't have started chasing him for that in the first place."

"I want two volunteers to stay here and watch over things until I can get back tomorrow with the sheriff and the coroner. They'll want to reconstruct how all this happened," Fitzgerald said.

Blair and Lathrop agreed to stay at the campsite while the others returned to report the grim findings.

"Keep an eye peeled," Fitzgerald told the pair as he prepared to lead the other posse members out to civilization. "I don't think Tornow will be back. Looks like he's taken most of his venison jerky and other belongings and moved away from here. But watch out anyway, I'll see you tomorrow."

* * *

Sheriff Payette and Coroner French hiked into the remote murder scene the next day. A posse brought out the bodies of the two deputies.

Within days, the commissioners increased the reward money to $4,000, and Washington's Governor Hay, added another $1,000. The reward offering was split, $3,000 for the capture of John Tornow, dead or alive, and $2,000 for the conviction of the killer of either the Bauer twins or McKenzie and Elmer. This posting further indicated the law's uncertainty that John had killed the Bauer twins. The evidence was stronger that he had murdered the two deputies. Innocent or guilty, the $5,000 price put on John's head, equivalent to $75,000 in today's dollars, made him a sought after fugitive.

Before long, many reports flowed into the sheriff's office claiming Tornow had been seen all over Washington State. One "eye-witness" account claimed John had been wounded in a saloon brawl in Seattle, but had escaped by jumping onto a streetcar.

A woman who was supposed to have known Tornow quite well—it was never determined where or how she had met him—told officers she had seen him walking through the streets of Port Angeles. A newspaper reporter wrote an article claiming John had fathered a child then abandoned the mother in Portland. But oldtimers who knew John scoffed at all these rumored sightings. "He's right up there in the wilderness he loves so much," one homesteader said, "and I ain't so sure John's really guilty of all these terrible things he's being accused of."

Deputy Colin McKenzie and game warden A.V. Elmer were given hero's funerals and eulogized for their valor. A bronze plaque commemorating their bravery was placed in the marble corridor of the new Chehalis county (now Grays Harbor county) courthouse in Montesano. It reads: "They died without hope of reward." The memoriam remains there today as a reminder to younger generations of the unselfish heroism shown by these two men.

* * *

Following the murders, John Tornow piled his meager belongings into his packsack, loaded a second one taken from McKenzie, took what dried elk venison he could carry and made a frantic dash deeper into the isolated interior of the Olympics. Some said his brain and thought processes now became irrational. In short, it was quite possible the violent actions and tremendous pressures incurred were literally causing him cerebral short-circuiting.

In all likelihood, John's sight was probably blurred by the reoccurring vision of the two dead deputies sprawled amidst the blood on the mossy forest floor. Like a subliminal picture rapidly flashed on the mirror of his mind, that nightmare-scape kept repeating, over and over again, haunting his memory.

As if trying to escape his own mental persecution, surrendering to impulse, with reckless abandon he crashed through the thick

186

Plaque honoring deputies McKenzie and Elmer who were murdered in the wilderness by John Tornow in 1912. It is inscribed "They died without hope of reward."

underbrush. He became oblivious to trails or shortcuts as he fled the death scene. Seeing nothing but the haunting faces of the two deputies in death, the forest loner tripped over fallen logs, became entangled in thorny blackberry vines, caroomed off huge tree trunks. He tried to escape from the tormenting voice of the past. But he couldn't outrun it; couldn't erase it from his mind; couldn't control his thought processes. Like a man possessed, unseeing he fled directionless through the woodlands.

The driving influence behind John's pell-mell flight was his inner-voice repeating, *Run, John, run. Run, John, run.* After several hours, downright exhausted, so drained he no longer had the strength to stand, he collapsed like a stringless puppet, falling to the spruce needle cushion of the forest floor. Laying there, he sobbed pitifully, reduced to the mental state of an infant.

* * *

Twittering birds and blossoming flora accompanied the spring season in western Washington State. During that same month, on April 14, 1912, the world was stunned by the sinking of the Titanic and resultant heavy loss of life.

In a frantic attempt to bring John Tornow to justice, or at least question him about the murders, Sheriff Payette himself led several prolonged searches into the upper Satsop and Wynooche watersheds. Each time, the posses returned even more frustrated than the time before. All they found were cold campfires, abandoned hideouts, and faded, weeks-old tracks in dried mud that may or may not have been made by John Tornow. The law was no closer to apprehending him than when the manhunt had begun eight months earlier. They were pursuing a wilderness magician; almost an illusionist, a quarry who was like a skilled professional in his natural habitat, while his pursuers appeared as amateurs.

"John might be somewhat befuddled in his head, but it has only sharpened his cunning and elusiveness," Sheriff Payette was heard to mutter.

However, at the same time, John was being pressured to remain always alert. The comparatively huge reward for his apprehension compelled all types of would-be bounty hunters to plunge headlong into the wilderness. For some, the sizeable payoff spawned dreams of a rich retirement.

Sheriff Payette issued bulletins and printed warnings about the dangers associated with pursuing the forest loner. "Being an expert rifleman and skilled outdoorsman are not the sole prerequisites for capturing Tornow," he stated. "His cunning ability to elude searchers has been honed to a razor's edge through many years of wilderness experience. I doubt any man possesses the survival and elusiveness skills of this fugitive. Be forewarned, he's armed and can be very dangerous."

The reputation of the so-called, "Wild Man of the Oxbow," and Payette's warning, almost a pleading, were not enough to dissuade adventuresome thrill-seekers from entering the forest in search of the fugitive. Nobody will ever know if, or how many men may have fallen victim to John's now-turned violent impatience with harassing pursuers. Fifteen to twenty men were thought to have entered the wilderness at various times in search of him. Some were never seen again. Anyone of the era who wished to vanish and start a new life had just to announce they were going in search of John Tornow.

Sheriff Payette confirmed a disappearance that he deemed very suspicious. "I understand that Paddy McHugh, a well-known Hoquiam saloonkeeper had grubstaked two prospectors, 'Scotty,' and, 'The Swede.' The two men were reported entering the Olympic Mountains in search of gold and were never seen again. Seems unusual to me that two prospectors could just disappear like that."

* * *

There was a loud noise, sounded like a rifle shot, in the Bauer homestead yard. Minnie smiled with joy as she looked out and saw John Kennedy climbing down from his automobile. She hadn't seen him for a couple of weeks and now looked forward to deepening their relationship.

She met him on the front porch with a platonic kiss and a warm embrace. "Hello, Minnie," he smiled, "you look stunning as usual."

"It's wonderful to see you again," she purred. "Come in and sit for a spell, I'll put the coffee pot on."

Sliding a chair out from the table as Minnie busied herself putting the blue-enamel pot on the stove, Kennedy said, "I was sorry to hear they're laying the blame on your brother for the murder of those two deputies."

"I dunno what to think," she said, shoving another piece of wood onto the cookstove's glowing red coals. "I'm afraid maybe they've went too far. They blamed John for what happened to my boys when in my heart I know he ain't guilty. Now them two lawmen. Maybe he just got aggravated with the way they're puttin' all this on him and he fought back. Maybe, I dunno."

"Well I hope they bring him in without harm so this can all be sorted out," Kennedy said. He helped Minnie by taking two cups down from the cupboard and setting them on the table as he spoke. "More for your peace of mind than anything else. Your comfort is my main concern."

"You make me feel good when you say that," she smiled at him.

"Reason I stopped by, other than to see you again. I wanted to ask you to go to the Matlock Grange social with me tomorrow night. A lot of our neighbors will be there, it will be potluck and should be a lot of fun. Will you go?"

Pouring the coffee, Minnie almost missed the cups, spilling on the ivory-colored lace tablecloth. This was the first time John had asked her out. What would people think, seeing them together? Was it too soon? Henry's been gone less than a year. He should have disappeared long ago. These minor negative thoughts were insufficient to sway her. "Oh, John, that sounds like fun. Sure I'll go with you."

The Matlock Grange was first formed in 1910 as the Lincoln Grange and was the social meeting hub of the Matlock area. It included the small settlements of Deckerville, Beeville, Little Egypt and Frisken Wye, a tucked away railroad settlement. Minnie was skittish as a teenager as she began fussing and primping for the evening out with John Kennedy. Her first social event in more years than she could remember, especially with a man. Especially with a man the likes of Kennedy.

Bubbling to herself, she thought, this is a wonderful time to get all gussied up and wear my new dress again. She was ready to go and it was much too early. John said he'd pick her up at seven. A glance at the gold time piece on the wall confirmed it was only six-thirty.

In awhile, Minnie heard the Reo's backfire and raced to the front door; she no longer worried about appearing too anxious—it showed and she didn't care. There he stood, nattily attired in a freshly pressed gray suit, matching necktie and a charcoal Homburg hat. He presented her with a bright corsage of multiple spring flowers. "Good evening, Minnie," the timber baron smiled at her.

Seeing the corsage brought a tear tumbling down Minnie's cheek. "Oh John, you surely do spoil me, thank you so much."

Minnie had baked a chocolate cake for the potluck. Now, she was careful to set it on the floor of the Reo as Kennedy held the door open for her.

Other couples were also just arriving as they pulled up at the grange hall. W. F. Valley, Grange Secretary, greeted them at the door and Kennedy introduced Minnie to the Grange Master, Joseph Carstairs and his wife. "So nice you could join us," she smiled at Minnie.

The people were cordial to her that night. Although heads turned to admire her and Kennedy, nobody mentioned Henry Bauer. Nobody brought up the subject of her brother John Tornow, even though Minnie knew it was on everyone's mind.

Taking Minnie home after the enjoyable social event, Kennedy pulled into the rutted dirt yard, not much needing the vehicle's faint headlights to see the road. The countryside was bathed in brilliance from a full moon in a cloudless sky. Every tree and stump on the nearby hills stood out in full detail as if it were midday.

Turning off the ignition, Kennedy waited for the predictable bang before he slid over and gently encircled Minnie with his right arm. The timber baron kissed her with unusual warmth and passion, like he'd never kissed her before. Wow! Minnie thought, I ain't been kissed like that since little Jimmy Ford smooched me in the sixth grade behind the schoolhouse wood pile.

Smiling his best, eyes twinkling in the lustrous moonlight, Kennedy went around and opened the car door for her. With a bow and a flourish, he swung the door wide, declaring, "For your pleasure, madame. May I escort you to your abode?" Minnie giggled, "You sure can, John." Arm in arm the couple minced across the yard, entered the house, and with a gentle nudge, closed the door behind them. Quietness descended on the small moonlit farm home.

* * *

During the warm weather of summer and autumn of 1912, Sheriff Payette intensified the hunt for John Tornow in the Olympics. It was a huge and rugged country, ideal for an experienced fugitive to elude his pursuers.

John had an uncanny sixth sense that told him where to hide, or more importantly, where not to hide. He also knew which homesteaders were his friends, could be trusted. He covertly visited outlying farms, whether occupants were home or not, obtaining foodstuffs to vary his monotonous wilderness diet. On occasion, local residents found produce missing from their root cellars, but in trade would be a quarter of a deer or elk. They knew John had paid them a visit once again. There exists no records that he threatened or coerced any of the residents. More often they supported his fugitive role and were glad to share what food they had with him. Like a forest ghost, John left no trail whenever his wanderings touched the fringes of civilization. He drifted in very quiet, unannounced, and departed furtively, like a cunning fox, before anyone realized he had been there.

* * *

The line of deputies twenty-strong advanced with rifles blazing, held at belt-buckle height. Bullets whizzed all around him, cutting limbs and kicking up dirt but miraculously missing him. Although John slept through this nightmare, the inexorable inner-voice woke him at last. *Run, John, run. Run, John, run.*

The fugitive, now with long stringy hair to his shoulders and a full black beard, arose with a frightened jolt from his deep moss bed in a rustic slab lean-to. Jumping up, he raced outside and began surveying his immediate surroundings—no deputies, no blazing rifles, no bullets—it had just been another nightmare, one in a long series that often interrupted his attempts to rest. And the little voice just laughed in his ears. John's screams were aimed upwards to the forest treetops and scared a pair of mountain bluebirds resting among the green foliage of an Oregon ash above his well-concealed hideout. "Leave me alone," he implored, arms outstretched to the heavens. "Quit eatin' away at me, you're drivin' me crazy."

* * *

In late fall, majestic V's of Canadian honkers bound for warmer regions passed overhead one after another; their mellifluous cries flowing gentle in their wake.

Autumn faded into a blustery winter with storm after storm churning in off the Pacific Ocean. The weather hit Washington's Olympic peninsula full tilt in her forested uplands. The harsh winds carpeted the forest floor with fallen deciduous leaves. John prepared to spend his second winter in the wilds; fifteen months since he'd seen his sister Minnie, a long time to live off the land with limited civilized food or niceties. Although not of great importance to him, he had talked with few people during most of those months. He'd only conversed with the trees and mountains, once in a while a bird, squirrel or a timid deer. Oh, how he yearned to see and talk with his loving Sister.

The advent of winter also worried Sheriff Ed Payette. He'd led numerous posses in search of John Tornow but had returned empty-handed. He hadn't even come close to capturing the fugitive in this one-sided game of cat-and-mouse. His bosses, the county commissioners, were less than satisfied with the ever-increasing manpower expenses that had provided no results. They threatened to slash the sheriff's operating budget.

Prior to the fall elections, Schelle Mathews, a young blacksmith from the small town of Elma who had once worked as a deputy, decided to run for Sheriff Payette's job. He campaigned on a platform promising to bring John Tornow to justice. It seemed that public sentiment, at least from the urban sector, was beginning to run high for John's capture. Predicated on his vow to apprehend the forest loner, Mathews was voted into office as Chehalis county Sheriff, officially taking the helm on January 13, 1913.

Undaunted by the winter weather, the new sheriff at once organized a posse and struck out after Tornow through the deep snows of the Olympics. The men returned after a week or so; tired, wet and very disillusioned about snaring the, "Wildman of the Oxbow." Mathews mounted several more searches, bagging only what snipe hunters bring home—an empty sack.

* * *

By early spring of 1913, a warming trend began to thaw the cold mantle of winter. It melted the deep snows, brought back the birds and animals from the lowlands to the Olympic foothills.

John Tornow, now thirty-two years old, had been a wanted fugitive for almost nineteen months. He looked like a fugitive; long stringy hair; hands and face darkened from the weather, campfires and wilderness grime; jagged dirt-encrusted finger-nails; tattered ragged clothes. He wore several garments at a time to cover holes, and had a smell about him that only a skunk would appreciate. He'd lived like an animal for most of those months—even some animals lived better.

John was still haunted by the inner-voice; only now he was beginning to talk back more often, "I don't care what you say, I ain't the one killed my nephews. Someone else done it."

Then one day John remembered the good times he'd enjoyed with his Pa at Frog Lake and decided to return. There was a tumbled-down lean-to shack on an island in the middle of the lake. I can hide out there, he thought to himself, ain't nobody knows 'bout that spot. Hide among the cattails and lily pads, with the frogs and the king-fishers and the herons.

So, on that fateful day in April, 1913, John made the decision to return to the place that held fond memories for him. Frog Lake was the place of his happy childhood, before threatening inner-voices, before men chased after him, before vague remembrances he had of blood, death and contorted faces.

At about this same time Sheriff Schelle Mathews was called to Tacoma as a witness in a federal court hearing. During the trip, John Tornow's fate was finalized by a casual, chance-in-a-million meeting between two men in the train's club car. Sheriff Mathews was enjoy-ing a drink and a cigar when Hoquiam land developer J.B. Lucas hap-pened to stroll in.

Recognizing the sheriff, Lucas sat down, introduced himself and began talking about the Tornow case.

"I was never altogether convinced that John killed his nephews. The one time I met and talked with him, he seemed like a reason-able sort. Even invited me to share his supper in camp one night," Lucas said.

"I agree there could be some doubt about him killing the Bauer twins," Mathews said, blowing a blue cloud of cigar smoke across the table. "But the evidence is quite conclusive he shot McKenzie and Elmer."

"Yes, can't argue much with that. But maybe all of us, the public in general, the law in particular, pushed him too hard, pushed him right off the thin edge of sanity," Lucas replied. "Did you ever think of that?"

Mathews bristled at the cutting remark but thought to himself that

The late Albert Kuhnle, upper Satsop Valley pioneer, led the author into Tornow Lake in 1963. He allegedly accompanied the posse to the lake in 1913 to help bring out the bodies of John Tornow and the two slain deputies.

Lucas might be somewhat correct. "Well, I agree with a little of what you say."

"I hate to even suggest this because I'm kind of on John's side," Lucas began, stroking his weathered chin while trying to decide if he wanted to help the sheriff's manhunt. "I once met John at a small lake up in the Oxbow country. He told me it was one of his favorite hangouts. He spent a lot of time there."

Recognizing that this tip could break the Tornow case for him, in eagerness Mathews asked, "Could you draw me a map to find that lake?"

"Sure thing," Lucas said, reaching for a fountain pen, "Got a piece of paper?"

"Use the back of this 'wanted' poster."

"If John's there, I hope he comes in without a fight. I'd like to see justice prevail and you get to the bottom of what, in fact, happened in those killings," Lucas explained as he began to write.

"My primary concern is to bring him in," Mathews said, casting a serious frown towards the land developer. "If he comes in agreeable, so much the better."

The train wheels hadn't even stopped rolling before the sheriff hurried down the coach steps. He leaped across the station platform and was on the phone to his trusted deputy and brother-in-law, Giles Quimby.

"Get a few of the boys together for a scouting party," he excitedly told Quimby. "Fellow gave me a map showing where he thinks Tornow might be holed up. I'll want you to go look around, determine if he might be there. If he is, we'll go in with a full posse and nail him. I'll be in the office tomorrow." Continuing, Mathews said, "Don't get too close to the lake. Just reconnoiter to see if there's any sign of life, then get the hell outta there."

The sheriff gave Quimby detailed instructions for finding the lake—Frog Lake, John's favorite place. The lake so full of memories. The lake where he and Pa had spent so many happy times together.

* * *

Lawman Giles Quimby watched the cautious strides of his two deputies, Charley Lathrop and Louie Blair as they sneaked down the trail. They were drawn to the telltale wisp of smoke spiralling up from the island in the lake. Once again Quimby felt the pangs of apprehension surging through his arrow-thin body. He knew Tornow was in the lean-to; he knew the deputies would try to take the outlaw; he knew there would be lethal action like in the war when his post had been overrun by enemy soldiers. The very thought of the perils brought goose bumps to his bare skin. But this time would be different. He had to go with them. He had to do it.

Charley's obedient Airedale, Chief, was following on his master's heels. Quimby dropped in behind the dog. Too bad the weather's so clear and quiet, the deputy thought to himself. We could sure use a noisy little rainstorm right now to cover the sound of our approach.

Quiet as a snowflake drifting to the ground, Quimby gave a gentle hiss to get his companion's attention. Using hand signals, he

197

called for a huddle and one last strategy session before reaching the island. He prayed that his anxiety wouldn't be noticeable as he spoke. In such a low whisper he could just hear it himself, he said, "If you guys are bound and determined to do this against my better judgement, we should at least split up so we don't give Tornow an easy target. I'll cover the left flank, Charley take the middle, Louie drift off to the right."

Without speaking, the deputies nodded their agreement. They were not as apprehensive as Quimby. But then they hadn't faced a company of Spanish soldiers charging at them with drawn sabers as he had.

In just a few minutes, the trail ended at a narrow foot-log that crossed about thirty feet of shallow water in front of the small island. The yellow bog moss carpeting the bridge-like log was worn down, showing signs of use as if someone had often walked on it.

As the men approached the water in total silence, the croaking of the frogs seemed deep-toned, getting louder as they approached. In apprehension, Louie stepped up on the log like he expected it to be booby-trapped. Charley followed, then Quimby. Chief bypassed the narrow bridge, instead wading the ankle-deep water, sidestepping the mare's-tail aquatic plants.

Taking just a couple of steps on the log, the deputies all of a sudden froze in motion. Something had changed. But what? Then they noticed the abrupt stillness. From instinct, the frogs had quit croaking as the men approached. Chief looked up at Charley. Even the dog was aware of the sudden silence. A foreboding, deathlike silence. If a pin had fallen, it would have sounded to them like an iron pipe.

* * *

John was enjoying the mid-morning spring sunshine that beamed down on the tiny island through the majestic spruce and fir trees that ringed the lake. He was frying a monotonous breakfast of sliced venison over his small campfire. He tried to keep the fire contained by burning red cedar to minimize smoke that might disclose his camp.

Out on the lake John watched a belted kingfisher fly a jerky route above the water. The bird's ragged, bushy topknot bounced sideways as the feathered fisher rattled it's shrill cry. Without warning, the blue-gray bird folded it's wings forming a slender missile and arrowed into the dark-blue lake after a minnow, bringing a smile to John's bearded face.

*　*　*

In an instant he heard it. He heard the silence of the frogs. His inner-voice panicked. *Run, John, run.* The forest loner reached for his Winchester which he'd reloaded from ammunition taken from one of the slain deputies. His black eyes rolled in wild gyrations, showing only whites under his dark, bushy eyebrows. He jumped behind a huge spruce tree twice the thickness of his scraggy body. John peered out where the access path approached his camp. He watched the dark trail opening like a cat watches a bird in a cage.

All of a sudden he saw them, two men and a dog, looked like lawmen. *Shoot 'em, kill 'em,* sounded the troublesome inner-voice. Gotta be careful, John thought to himself, careful not to hurt the dog.

Out of sight, Quimby had flanked off to the left, but Blair and Lathrop stayed almost together, a dangerous move.

A rifle shot shattered the silence, echoing and rolling across the quiet waters of the little lake. Shooting sightless, the fugitive had thrown the rifle to his shoulder and with uncanny accuracy sent a lethal bullet tearing open Louis Blair's chest and shredding his heart into bloody tendrils. Dead on his feet, the deputy collapsed lifeless onto the lake-shore grass, still wet from the morning mist.

At the bark of John's rifle, Lathrop leaped behind an old-growth Douglas fir. He shielded his body from the direction of the camp and held his rifle upright. The cold, steel barrel was right in front of his nose, a finger on the trigger ready to fire in a heartbeat. Tornow peered around the edge of the spruce. Where was the second lawman? He'd lost him, couldn't see him behind the tree. Then Lathrop edged out just enough to get off two shots that thunked into John's tree.

Peering from behind his spruce, exposing just his head to look for Lathrop, John saw him fire twice before the deputy slid back behind the fir. Tornow had him targeted. They were in front of the lean-to at close range. Waiting, watching patiently for his quarry to reappear, with just an inch or two of his head exposed, Tornow stood ready, biding his time, wanting just one clear shot.

Soon, Charley Lathrop made a disastrous mistake. He edged out ever so little from behind the fir, just enough to look for Tornow. He didn't expose much of his body for a target but it was all John needed. A well-placed shot sent a bolt of hot steel piercing the deputy's shoulder, smashing bones and rendering his left arm useless. He cried out in severe agony.

The impact of the thirty-calibre slug knocked Lathrop to the ground. His now prone body was exposed to Tornow's murderous fire. Spurting blood and near death, Lathrop managed to shoot three more volleys each time he saw Tornow's shaggy head appear from behind the tree. Almost unconscious, the deputy was laying in grass, dirt and fir needles. The forest debris soon jammed Lathrop's rifle before he could shoot again. In his exposed position, unable to fire, the deputy was an easy target for Tornow's last killing shot.

Meanwhile, Giles Quimby had been flanking the two deputies about thirty yards through the timber to their left side. He cursed as he saw them stay together rather than splitting up as he'd told them. It could have been a fatal mistake.

From his flanking position, Quimby dodged behind a tree and fired each time John's unkempt body became visible from around his shielding spruce tree.

Tornow continued shooting at the lifeless forms of Blair and Lathrop. It was assumed the fugitive thought Quimby's firing was coming from one of the dead deputies. All of a sudden the forest loner realized Quimby's bullets were thwacking into his tree from a different direction. He wondered. Could there have been three lawmen? They only sent two last time. With a fierce look on his bushy face, the fugitive turned to his right and for the first time spotted his third adversary.

Through the haze of gunsmoke, John Tornow's eyes now blazed with fury. It seemed the heat of battle had ignited a hatred which could only be appeased through the spilling of more blood.

All at once Quimby realized he was now the center of the outlaw's attention. He turned pale as the blood drained from his face in terror of going one-on-one with the "Wildman of the Oxbow." It was something he hadn't wanted to do from the very beginning.

The deputy checked his rifle, still loaded, the hammer back, ready to fire. In apprehension he dropped to one knee before edging out from behind the tree. Quimby thought Tornow might not spot him as easy if he was crouched. He only showed enough of his head for one eyeball to search for the outlaw. Where was he?

By now, the battle, the taunting inner-voice, the death and broken flesh had reduced John Tornow to an irrational, crazed outlaw. He'd taken a non-lethal hit to his upper body. It seemed to fuel his burning desire to stop his relentless pursuers. And perhaps now his brief impairment of sanity caused him to become more reckless.

In apprehension, Quimby searched for his target. In the flick of an eye he spotted the shaggy head peering at him around the side of the spruce tree. The deputy threw up his rifle. He filled the sights altogether with the outlaw's head. Then, with careful purpose Quimby squeezed off the shot. The head disappeared.

The lawman pulled back behind the tree and glanced down at his rifle. *Empty!* He'd fired his seventh and last bullet. Now it was dead-quiet. Not a sound. Risking a quick look, he couldn't see Tornow. Like the ghost he could become, was it possible the outlaw was at that very minute circling behind him to get in one last killing shot? Had Quimby's final bullet found the mark and the fugitive was laying dead behind the giant spruce? Could some run-of-the-mill deputy like him have put an end to the infamous John Tornow legend? Quimby's mind raced through all these possibilities, it raced out of control. Too many questions. Too few answers.

The deputy's survival instinct soon snapped him back to reality. At that very moment, the outlaw might be stalking him and there he stood with an empty rifle. He pulled several cartridges from his pocket and, fumbling, dropped them in the dirt. By his own published admission, Quimby began trembling so unrestrained he couldn't reload his rifle. He was frightened beyond comprehension, pale as a blank sheet of paper, almost frozen with fear.

The scene remained graveyard quiet. Quimby could see the bodies of his dead deputies, wondering to himself if he was soon to join them. Lathrop's Airedale stood silent vigil over his master's corpse.

And then he ran. Quimby's intuition told him to get out of there. Get far away. He ran out the trail, across the foot-log, slipping twice and falling flat into the shallow lake. But the cold water felt good to his hot, sweat-drenched body.

It was estimated that the logging camp was almost six miles from Frog Lake. The deputy ran all the way. He phoned Sheriff Mathews from the camp to tell him they'd stumbled onto Tornow's hideout. "I'm not sure if he's dead or not," Quimby stammered, still frightened from his terrible ordeal.

The next day, Quimby guided the sheriff and a large posse that had been recruited on the supposition the manhunt was not yet concluded, to Frog Lake. Chief continued to maintain his vigil over Lathrop's lifeless form.

John Tornow's disheveled body was discovered slumped behind the giant spruce tree, still clutching his rifle. He had been killed by a bullet that entered his neck and angled through his upper body. The longest manhunt in the forests of the Pacific Northwest had ended. From that day forward, Frog Lake became known as Tornow Lake, as it still is known today.

John Tornow was buried near his parents in the small community's Grove Cemetery, near the family homestead. That was also the final resting place for Mary Bauer and the Bauer twins, John and William.

Perhaps John's only transgressions were his immense desire towards solitary existence and his deep-rooted love of the outdoors. When others sought to remove him from his favored natural element, to deprive him of his right to choose, he resisted. Though unfortunate, John's love of solitude became greater than his aversion towards violence. At this point, his resistance turned homicidal.

The true story has been forever lost in the passing of those few individuals who knew the truth and carried it to their graves. We can only speculate.

After considerable litigation, Giles Quimby received the five-thousand dollar reward for ending Tornow's reign. He retired in Montesano until 1947 when he was hit and killed by a car in the small community's main intersection.

So, at last, the outlaw's wish had been granted; the "Wild Man of the Oxbow" remained forever at peace in the tree-lined cemetery near the wilderness he loved.

And Minnie Tornow Bauer? If fantasies come true, she married the author's fictional John Kennedy, her knight in shining armor, and lived happily ever after.

Epilogue

The last cartridge in Giles Quimby's rifle triggered the final chapter in the life of John Tornow. But beyond the finis of John's troubled years arose a multitude of uncertainties regarding the truth within the chronicles. Was he villain or victim? Mentally deficient or socially regressive? Innocent or guilty?

The forest loner might not have even been on stage when the turning point in his life-drama occurred. The murder of his beloved nephews, John and William Bauer, ignited the furor, right or wrong, that culminated in the legal killing of John Tornow.

His fate was sealed with the controversial reward posted for his apprehension, if only for questioning, in the murder of the Bauer twins.

For reasons of his own, he refused to return to civilization. And who could blame him? His reason, a dislike of humankind, had no connection whatsoever with the brutal murders.

And so the noose of circumstance began to tighten around John Tornow's neck. Having found a lean-to in the vicinity of the murders that was thought to have been used by the loner, Sheriff Payette identified him as the prime suspect. At that time, he announced that Tornow was sought just for questioning in the twins' murder.

Printed media jumped on the case, swaying public opinion through sensationalism against him. People unfamiliar with the circumstances hysterically pinned the guilt on John. Mental retardation was a little-known affliction in the early 1900's, and people then, as now, feared the unknown.

Important facts in the case were overlooked. John's fondness for his nephews was often demonstrated. Some even suggested John mistook the boys for someone else. Mistaken identity? Hardly. Poor eyesight blamed on a marksman who was rifle-accurate at hundreds of yards? Also, there was the love he felt for his sister Minnie who had nurtured him throughout the years. He would kill his sister's children? Never.

Law officials also disregarded the possibility there could be other suspects. And literally, the woods were full of them. There is not a shred of documentation that anyone, up to and including John Tornow, was ever brought in for questioning in connection with the murders of John and William Bauer. Perhaps in their haste and lacking more sophisticated criminal investigative techniques, lawmen of the era bypassed evidence that could have pointed towards other suspects. In addition, anyone seeking to profit from John's substantial bank account or land and timber holdings could have planned his demise through collusion with others or a frame-up for the murders.

John Tornow was tried in absentia around many dinner tables in Western Washington and found *Guilty by Circumstance* in the minds of the sheriff, news media, and townspeople.

The true story will never be known.